The Poems and Prose of Ernest Dowson

Ernest Dowson

Table of Contents

ERNEST DOWSON

I

The death of Ernest Dowson will mean very little to the world at large, but it will mean a great deal to the few people who care passionately for poetry. A little book of verses, the manuscript of another, a one-act play in verse, a few short stories, two novels written in collaboration, some translations from the French, done for money; that is all that was left by a man who was undoubtedly a man of genius, not a great poet, but a poet, one of the very few writers of our generation to whom that name can be applied in its most intimate sense. People will complain, probably, in his verses, of what will seem to them the factitious melancholy, the factitious idealism, and (peeping through at a few rare moments) the factitious suggestions of riot. They will see only a literary affectation, where in truth there is as genuine a note of personal sincerity as in the more explicit and arranged confessions of less admirable poets. Yes, in these few evasive, immaterial snatches of song, I find, implied for the most part, hidden away like a secret, all the fever and turmoil and the unattained dreams of a life which had itself so much of the swift, disastrous, and suicidal impetus of genius.

Ernest Christopher Dowson was born at The Grove, Belmont Hill, Lee, Kent, on August 2nd, 1867; he died at 26 Sandhurst Gardens, Catford, S.E., on Friday morning, February 23, 1900, and was buried in the Roman Catholic part of the Lewisham Cemetery on February 27. His great-uncle was Alfred Domett, Browning's "Waring," at one time Prime Minister of New Zealand, and author of "Ranolf and Amohia," and other poems. His father, who had himself a taste for literature, lived a good deal in France and on the Riviera, on account of the delicacy of his health, and Ernest had a somewhat irregular education, chiefly out of England, before he entered Queen's College, Oxford. He left in 1887 without taking a degree, and came to London, where he lived for several years, often revisiting France, which was always his favourite country. Latterly, until the last year of his life, he lived almost entirely in Paris, Brittany, and Normandy. Never robust, and always reckless with himself, his health had been steadily getting worse for some years, and when he came back to London he looked, as indeed he was, a dying man. Morbidly shy, with a sensitive independence which shrank from any sort of obligation, he would not communicate with his relatives, who would gladly have helped him, or with any of the really large number of attached friends whom he had in London; and, as his disease weakened him more and more, he hid himself away in his miserable lodgings, refused to see a doctor, let himself half starve, and was found one day in a Bodega with only a few shillings in his pocket, and so weak as to be hardly able to walk, by a friend, himself in some difficulties, who immediately took him back to the bricklayer's cottage in a muddy outskirt of Catford, where he was himself living, and there generously looked after him for the last six weeks of his life.

He did not realise that he was going to die; and was full of projects for the future, when the £600 which was to come to him from the sale of some property should have given him a fresh chance in the world; began to read Dickens, whom he had never read before, with singular zest; and, on the last day of his life, sat up talking eagerly till five in the morning. At the very moment of his death he did not know that he was dying. He tried to cough, could not cough, and the heart quietly stopped.

II

I cannot remember my first meeting with Ernest Dowson. It may have been in 1891, at one of the meetings of the Rhymers' Club, in an upper room of the "Cheshire Cheese," where long clay pipes lay in slim heaps on the wooden tables, between tankards of ale; and young poets, then very young, recited their own verses to one another with a desperate and ineffectual attempt to get into key with the Latin Quarter. Though few of us were, as a matter of fact, Anglo-Saxon, we could not help feeling that we were in London, and the atmosphere of London is not the atmosphere of movements or of societies. In Paris it is the most natural thing in the world to meet and discuss literature, ideas, one's own and one another's work; and it can be done without pretentiousness or constraint, because, to the Latin mind, art, ideas, one's work and the work of one's friends, are definite and important things, which it would never occur to any one to take anything but seriously. In England art has to be protected not only against the world, but against one's self and one's fellow artist, by a kind of affected modesty which is the Englishman's natural pose, half pride and half self-distrust. So this brave venture of the Rhymers' Club, though it lasted for two or three years, and produced two little books of verse which will some day be literary curiosities, was not quite a satisfactory kind of *cénacle*. Dowson, who enjoyed the real thing so much in Paris, did not, I think, go very often; but his contributions to the first book of the club were at once the most delicate and the most distinguished poems which it contained. Was it, after all, at one of these meetings that I first saw him, or was it, perhaps, at another haunt of some of us at that time, a semi-literary tavern near Leicester Square, chosen for its convenient position between two stage-doors? It was at the time when one or two of us sincerely worshipped the ballet; Dowson, alas! never. I could never get him to see that charm in harmonious and coloured movement, like bright shadows seen through the floating gauze of the music, which held me night after night at the two theatres which alone seemed to me to give an amusing colour to one's dreams. Neither the stage nor the stage-door had any attraction for him; but he came to the tavern because it was a tavern, and because he could meet his friends there. Even before that time I have a vague impression of having met him, I forget where, certainly at night; and of having been struck, even then, by a look and manner of pathetic charm, a sort of Keats-like face, the face of a demoralised Keats, and by something curious in the contrast of a manner exquisitely refined, with an appearance generally somewhat dilapidated. That impression was only accentuated later on, when I came to know him, and the manner of his life, much more intimately.

I think I may date my first impression of what one calls "the real man" (as if it were more real than the poet of the disembodied verses!) from an evening in which he first introduced me to those charming supper-houses, open all night through, the cabmen's shelters. I had been talking over another vagabond poet, Lord Rochester, with a charming and sympathetic descendant of that poet, and somewhat late at night we had come upon Dowson and another man wandering aimlessly and excitedly about the streets. He invited us to supper, we did not quite realise where, and the cabman came in with us, as we were welcomed, cordially and without comment, at a little place near the Langham; and, I recollect, very hospitably entertained. The cooking differs, as I found in time, in these supper-houses, but there the rasher was excellent and the cups admirably clean. Dowson was known there, and I used to think he was always at his best in a cabmen's shelter. Without a certain sordidness in his surroundings he was never quite comfortable, never quite himself; and at those places you are obliged to drink nothing stronger than coffee or tea. I liked to see him occasionally, for a change, drinking nothing stronger than coffee or tea. At Oxford, I believe, his favourite form of intoxication had been haschisch; afterwards he gave up this somewhat elaborate experiment in visionary sensations for readier means of oblivion; but he returned to it, I remember, for at least one afternoon, in a company of which I had been the gatherer and of which I was the host. I remember him sitting a little anxiously, with his chin on his breast, awaiting the magic, half-shy in the midst of a bright company of young people whom he had only seen across the footlights. The experience was not a very successful one; it ended in what should have been its first symptom, immoderate laughter.

Always, perhaps, a little consciously, but at least always sincerely, in search of new sensations, my friend found what was for him the supreme sensation in a very passionate and tender adoration of the most escaping of all ideals, the ideal of youth. Cherished, as I imagine, first only in the abstract, this search after the immature, the ripening graces which time can only spoil in the ripening, found itself at the journey's end, as some of his friends thought, a little prematurely. I was never of their opinion. I only saw twice, and for a few moments only, the young girl to whom most of his verses were to be written, and whose presence in his life may be held to account for much of that astonishing contrast between the broad outlines of his life and work. The situation seemed to me of the most exquisite and appropriate impossibility. The daughter of a refugee, I believe of good family, reduced to keeping a humble restaurant in a foreign quarter of London, she listened to his verses, smiled charmingly, under her mother's eyes, on his two years' courtship, and at the end of two years married the waiter instead. Did she ever realise more than the obvious part of what was being offered to her, in this shy and eager devotion? Did it ever mean very much to her to have made and to have killed a poet? She had, at all events, the gift of evoking, and, in its way, of retaining, all that was most delicate, sensitive, shy, typically poetic, in a nature which I can only compare to a weedy garden, its grass trodden down by many feet, but with one small, carefully tended flowerbed, luminous with lilies. I used to think, sometimes, of Verlaine and his "girl-wife," the one really profound passion, certainly, of that passionate career; the charming, child-like creature, to whom he looked back, at the end of his life, with an unchanged tenderness and disappointment: "Vous n'avez rien compris à ma simplicité," as he lamented. In the case of Dowson, however, there was a sort of virginal devotion, as to a Madonna; and I think, had things gone happily, to a conventionally happy ending, he would have felt (dare I say?) that his ideal had been spoilt.

But, for the good fortune of poets, things rarely do go happily with them, or to conventionally happy endings. He used to dine every night at the little restaurant, and I can always see the picture, which I have so often seen through the window in passing: the narrow room with the rough tables, for the most part empty, except in the innermost corner, where Dowson would sit with that singularly sweet and singularly pathetic smile on his lips (a smile which seemed afraid of its right to be there, as if always dreading a rebuff), playing his invariable after-dinner game of cards. Friends would come in during the hour before closing time; and the girl, her game of cards finished, would quietly disappear, leaving him with hardly more than the desire to kill another night as swiftly as possible.

Meanwhile she and the mother knew that the fragile young man who dined there so quietly every day way apt to be quite another sort of person after he had been three hours outside. It was only when his life seemed to have been irretrievably ruined that Dowson quite deliberately abandoned himself to that craving for drink, which was doubtless lying in wait for him in his blood, as consumption was also; it was only latterly, when he had no longer any interest in life, that he really wished to die. But I have never known him when he could resist either the desire or the consequences of drink. Sober, he was the most gentle, in manner the most gentlemanly of men; unselfish to a fault, to the extent of weakness; a delightful companion, charm itself. Under the influence of drink, he became almost literally insane, certainly quite irresponsible. He fell into furious and unreasoning passions; a vocabulary unknown to him at other times sprang up like a whirlwind; he seemed always about to commit some act of absurd violence. Along with that forgetfulness came other memories. As long as he was conscious of himself, there was but one woman for him in the world, and for her he had an infinite tenderness and an infinite respect. When that face faded from him, he saw all the other faces, and he saw no more difference than between sheep and sheep. Indeed, that curious love of the sordid, so common an affectation of the modern decadent, and with him so genuine, grew upon him, and dragged him into more and more sorry corners of a life which was never exactly "gay" to him. His father, when he died, left him in possession of an old dock, where for a time he lived in a mouldering house, in that squalid part of the East End which he came to know so well, and to feel so strangely at home in. He drank the poisonous liquors of those pot-houses which swarm about the docks; he drifted about in whatever company came in his way; he let heedlessness develop into a curious disregard of personal tidiness. In Paris, Les Halles took the place of the docks. At Dieppe, where I saw so much, of him one summer, he discovered strange, squalid haunts about the harbour, where he made friends with amazing innkeepers, and got into rows with the fishermen who came in to drink after midnight. At Brussels, where I was with him at the time of the Kermesse, he flung himself into all that riotous Flemish life, with a zest for what was most sordidly riotous in it. It was his own way of escape from life.

To Dowson, as to all those who have not been "content to ask unlikely gifts in vain," nature, life, destiny, whatever one chooses to call it, that power which is strength to the strong, presented itself as a barrier against which all one's strength only served to dash one to more hopeless ruin. He was not a dreamer; destiny passes by the dreamer, sparing him because he clamours for nothing. He was a child, clamouring for so many things, all impossible. With a body too weak for ordinary existence, he desired all the enchantments of all the senses. With a soul too shy to tell its own secret, except in exquisite evasions, he desired the boundless confidence of love. He sang one tune, over and over, and no one listened to him. He had only to form the most simple wish, and it was denied him. He gave way to ill-luck, not knowing that he was giving way to his own weakness, and he tried to escape from the consciousness of things as they were at the best, by voluntarily choosing to accept them at their worst. For with him it was always voluntary. He was never quite without money; he had a little money of his own, and he had for many years a weekly allowance from a publisher, in return for translations from the French, or, if he chose to do it, original work. He was unhappy, and he dared not think. To unhappy men, thought, if it can be set at work on abstract questions, is the only substitute for happiness; if it has not strength to overleap the barrier which shuts one in upon oneself, it is the one unwearying torture. Dowson had exquisite sensibility, he vibrated in harmony with every delicate emotion; but he had no outlook, he had not the escape of intellect. His only escape, then, was to plunge into the crowd, to fancy that he lost sight of himself as he disappeared from the sight of others. The more he soiled himself at that gross contact, the further would he seem to be from what beckoned to him in one vain illusion after another vain illusion, in the delicate places of the world. Seeing himself moving to the sound of lutes, in some courtly disguise, down an alley of Watteau's Versailles, while he touched finger-tips with a divine creature in rose-leaf silks, what was there left for him, as the dream obstinately refused to realise itself, but a blind flight into some Teniers kitchen, where boors are making merry, without thought of yesterday or to-morrow? There, perhaps, in that ferment of animal life, he could forget life as he dreamed it, with too faint hold upon his dreams to make dreams come true.

For, there is not a dream which may not come true, if we have the energy which makes, or chooses, our own fate. We can always, in this world, get what we want, if we will it intensely and persistently enough. Whether we shall get it sooner or later is the concern of fate; but we shall get it. It may come when we have no longer any use for it, when we have gone on willing it out of habit, or so as not to confess that we have failed. But it will come. So few people succeed greatly because so few people can conceive a great end, and work towards that end without deviating and without tiring. But we all know that the man who works for money day and night gets rich; and the man who works day and night for no matter what kind of material power, gets the power. It is the same with the deeper, more spiritual, as it seems vaguer issues, which make for happiness and every intangible success. It is only the dreams of those light sleepers who dream faintly that do not come true.

We get out of life, all of us, what we bring to it; that, and that only, is what it can teach us. There are men whom Dowson's experiences would have made great men, or great writers; for him they did very little. Love and regret, with here and there the suggestion of an uncomforting pleasure snatched by the way, are all that he has to sing of; and he could have sung of them at much less "expense of spirit," and, one fancies, without the "waste of shame" at all. Think what Villon got directly out of his own life, what Verlaine, what Musset, what Byron, got directly out of their own lives! It requires a strong man to "sin strongly" and profit by it. To Dowson the tragedy of his own life could only have resulted in an elegy. "I have flung roses, roses, riotously with the throng," he confesses in his most beautiful poem; but it was as one who flings roses in a dream, as he passes with shut eyes through an unsubstantial throng. The depths into which he plunged were always waters of oblivion, and he returned forgetting them. He is always a very ghostly lover, wandering in a land of perpetual twilight, as he holds a whispered *colloque sentimental* with the ghost of an old love:

"Dans le vieux parc solitaire et glacé,
Deux spectres ont évoqué le passé."

It was, indeed, almost a literal unconsciousness, as of one who leads two lives, severed from one another as completely as sleep is from waking. Thus we get in his work very little of the personal appeal of those to whom riotous living, misery, a cross destiny, have been of so real a value. And it is important to draw this distinction, if only for the benefit of those young men who are convinced that the first step towards genius is disorder. Dowson is precisely one of the people who are pointed out as confirming this theory. And yet Dowson was precisely one of those who owed least to circumstances; and, in succumbing to them, he did no more than succumb to the destructive forces which, shut up within him, pulled down the house of life upon his own head.

A soul "unspotted from the world," in a body which one sees visibly soiling under one's eyes; that improbability is what all who knew him saw in Dowson, as his youthful physical grace gave way year by year, and the personal charm underlying it remained unchanged. There never was a simpler or more attaching charm, because there never was a sweeter or more honest nature. It was not because he ever said anything particularly clever or particularly interesting, it was not because he gave you ideas, or impressed you by any strength or originality, that you liked to be with him; but because of a certain engaging quality, which seemed unconscious of itself, which was never anxious to be or to do anything, which simply existed, as perfume exists in a flower. Drink was like a heavy curtain, blotting out everything of a sudden; when the curtain lifted, nothing had changed. Living always that double life, he had his true and his false aspect, and the true life was the expression of that fresh, delicate, and uncontaminated nature which some of us knew in him, and which remains for us, untouched by the other, in every line that he wrote.

III

Dowson was the only poet I ever knew who cared more for his prose than his verse; but he was wrong, and it is not by his prose that he will live, exquisite as that prose was at its best. He wrote two novels in collaboration with Mr. Arthur Moore: "A Comedy of Masks," in 1893, and "Adrian Rome," in 1899, both done under the influence of Mr. Henry James, both interesting because they were personal studies, and studies of known surroundings, rather than for their actual value as novels. A volume of "Stories and Studies in Sentiment," called "Dilemmas," in which the influence of Mr. Wedmore was felt in addition to the influence of Mr. James, appeared in 1895. Several other short stories, among his best work in prose, have not yet been reprinted from the *Savoy*. Some translations from the French, done as hack-work, need not be mentioned here, though they were never without some traces of his peculiar quality of charm in language. The short stories were indeed rather "studies in sentiment" than stories; studies of singular delicacy, but with only a faint hold on life, so that perhaps the best of them was not unnaturally a study in the approaches of death: "The Dying of Francis Donne." For the most part they dealt with the same motives as the poems, hopeless and reverent love, the ethics of renunciation, the disappointment of those who are too weak or too unlucky to take what they desire. They have a sad and quiet beauty of their own, the beauty of second thoughts and subdued emotions, of choice and scholarly English, moving in the more fluid and reticent harmonies of prose almost as daintily as if it were moving to the measure of verse. Dowson's care over English prose was like that of a Frenchman writing his own language with the respect which Frenchmen pay to French. Even English things had to come to him through France, if he was to prize them very highly; and there is a passage in "Dilemmas" which I have always thought very characteristic of his own tastes, as it refers to an "infinitesimal library, a few French novels, an Horace, and some well-thumbed volumes of the modern English poets in the familiar edition of Tauchnitz." He was Latin by all his affinities, and that very quality of slightness, of parsimony almost in his dealings with life and the substance of art, connects him with the artists of Latin races, who have always been so fastidious in their rejection of mere nature, when it comes too nakedly or too clamorously into sight and hearing, and so gratefully content with a few choice things faultlessly done.

And Dowson, in his verse (the "Verses" of 1896, "The Pierrot of the Minute," a dramatic phantasy in one act, of 1897, the posthumous volume "Decorations"), was the same scrupulous artist as in his prose, and more felicitously at home there. He was quite Latin in his feeling for youth, and death, and "the old age of roses," and the pathos of our little hour in which to live and love; Latin in his elegance, reticence, and simple grace in the treatment of these motives; Latin, finally, in his sense of their sufficiency for the whole of one's mental attitude. He used the commonplaces of poetry frankly, making them his own by his belief in them: the Horatian Cynara or Neobule was still the natural symbol for him when he wished to be most personal. I remember his saying to me that his ideal of a line of verse was the line of Poe:

"The viol, the violet, and the vine";

and the gracious, not remote or unreal beauty, which clings about such words and such images as these, was always to him the true poetical beauty. There never was a poet to whom verse came more naturally, for the song's sake; his theories were all æsthetic, almost technical ones, such as a theory, indicated by his preference for the line of Poe, that the letter "v" was the most beautiful of the letters, and could never be brought into verse too often. For any more abstract theories he had neither tolerance nor need. Poetry as a philosophy did not exist for him; it existed solely as the loveliest of the arts. He loved the elegance of Horace, all that was most complex in the simplicity of Poe, most birdlike in the human melodies of Verlaine. He had the pure lyric gift, unweighted or unballasted by any other quality of mind or emotion; and a song, for him, was music first, and then whatever you please afterwards, so long as it suggested, never told, some delicate sentiment, a sigh or a caress; finding words, at times, as perfect as the words of a poem headed, "O Mors! quam amara est memoria tua homini pacem habenti in substantiis suis."

There, surely, the music of silence speaks, if it has ever spoken. The words seem to tremble back into the silence which their whisper has interrupted, but not before they have created for us a mood, such a mood as the Venetian Pastoral of Giorgione renders in painting. Languid, half inarticulate, coming from the heart of a drowsy sorrow very conscious of itself, and not less sorrowful because it sees its own face looking mournfully back out of the water, the song seems to have been made by some fastidious amateur of grief, and it has all the sighs and tremors of the mood, wrought into a faultless strain of music. Stepping out of a paradise in which pain becomes so lovely, he can see the beauty which is the other side of madness, and, in a sonnet, "To One in Bedlam," can create a more positive, a more poignant mood, with fine subtlety.

Here, in the moment's intensity of this comradeship with madness, observe how beautiful the whole thing becomes; how instinctively the imagination of the poet turns what is sordid into a radiance, all stars and flowers and the divine part of forgetfulness! It is a symbol of the two sides of his own life: the side open to the street, and the side turned away from it, where he could "hush and bless himself with silence." No one ever worshipped beauty more devoutly, and just as we see him here transfiguring a dreadful thing with beauty, so we shall see, everywhere in his work, that he never admitted an emotion which he could not so transfigure. He knew his limits only too well; he knew that the deeper and graver things of life were for the most part outside the circle of his magic; he passed them by, leaving much of himself unexpressed, because he would not permit himself to express nothing imperfectly, or according to anything but his own conception of the dignity of poetry. In the lyric in which he has epitomised himself and his whole life, a lyric which is certainly one of the greatest lyrical poems of our time, "Non sum qualis eram bonae sub regno Cynarae," he has for once said everything, and he has said it to an intoxicating and perhaps immortal music.

Here, perpetuated by some unique energy of a temperament rarely so much the master of itself, is the song of passion and the passions, at their eternal war in the soul which they quicken or deaden, and in the body which they break down between them. In the second book, the book of "Decorations," there are a few pieces which repeat, only more faintly, this very personal note. Dowson could never have developed; he had already said, in his first book of verse, all that he had to say. Had he lived, had he gone on writing, he could only have echoed himself; and probably it would have been the less essential part of himself; his obligation to Swinburne, always evident, increasing as his own inspiration failed him. He was always without ambition, writing to please his own fastidious taste, with a kind of proud humility in his attitude towards the public, not expecting or requiring recognition. He died obscure, having ceased to care even for the delightful labour of writing. He died young, worn out by what was never really life to him, leaving a little verse which has the pathos of things too young and too frail ever to grow old.

ARTHUR SYMONS. 1900.

THE POEMS OF ERNEST DOWSON

TO MISSIE (A. P.)

IN PREFACE: FOR ADELAIDE

To you, who are my verses, as on some very future day, if you ever care to read them, you will understand, would it not be somewhat trivial to dedicate any one verse, as I may do, in all humility, to my friends? Trivial, too, perhaps, only to name you even here? Trivial, presumptuous? For I need not write your name for you at least to know that this and all my work is made for you in the first place, and I need not to be reminded by my critics that I have no silver tongue such as were fit to praise you. So for once you shall go indedicate, if not quite anonymous; and I will only commend my little book to you in sentences far beyond my poor compass which will help you perhaps to be kind to it:

"_Votre personne, vos moindres mouvements me semblaient avoir dans le monde une importance extrahumaine. Mon coeur comme de la poussière se soulevait derrière vos pas. Vous me faisiez l'effet d'un clair-de-lune par une nuit d'été, quand tout est parfums, ombres douces, blancheurs, infini; et les délices de la chair et de l'âme étaient contenues pour moi dans votre nom que je me répétais en tachant de le baiser sur mes lèvres.

"Quelquefois vos paroles me reviennent comme un écho lointain, comme le son d'une cloche apporté par le vent; et il me semble que vous êtes là quand je lis des passages de l'amour dans les livres.... Tout ce qu'on y blâme d'exagéré, vous me l'avez fait ressentir._"

PONT-AVEN, FINISTÈRE, 1896.

VERSES

Vitae summa brevis spem nos vetat incohare longam
They are not long, the weeping and the laughter.
Love and desire and hate:
I think they have no portion in us after
We pass the gate.
They are not long, the days of wine and roses:
Out of a misty dream
Our path emerges for a while, then closes
Within a dream.

A CORONAL

WITH HIS SONGS AND HER DAYS TO HIS LADY AND TO LOVE

Violets and leaves of vine,
Into a frail, fair wreath
We gather and entwine:
A wreath for Love to wear,
Fragrant as his own breath,
To crown his brow divine,
All day till night is near.
Violets and leaves of vine
We gather and entwine.

Violets and leaves of vine
For Love that lives a day,
We gather and entwine.
All day till Love is dead,
Till eve falls, cold and gray,
These blossoms, yours and mine,
Love wears upon his head,
Violets and leaves of vine
We gather and entwine.

Violets and leaves of vine,
For Love when poor Love dies
We gather and entwine.
This wreath that lives a day
Over his pale, cold eyes,
Kissed shut by Proserpine,
At set of sun we lay:
Violets and leaves of vine
We gather and entwine.

NUNS OF THE PERPETUAL ADORATION

Calm, sad, secure; behind high convent walls,
These watch the sacred lamp, these watch and pray:
And it is one with them when evening falls,
And one with them the cold return of day.

These heed not time; their nights and days they make
Into a long, returning rosary,
Whereon their lives are threaded for Christ's sake;
Meekness and vigilance and chastity.

A vowed patrol, in silent companies,
Life-long they keep before the living Christ.
In the dim church, their prayers and penances
Are fragrant incense to the Sacrificed.

Outside, the world is wild and passionate;
Man's weary laughter and his sick despair
Entreat at their impenetrable gate:
They heed no voices in their dream of prayer.

They saw the glory of the world displayed;
They saw the bitter of it, and the sweet;
They knew the roses of the world should fade,
And be trod under by the hurrying feet.

Therefore they rather put away desire,
And crossed their hands and came to sanctuary
And veiled their heads and put on coarse attire:
Because their comeliness was vanity.

And there they rest; they have serene insight
Of the illuminating dawn to be:
Mary's sweet Star dispels for them the night,
The proper darkness of humanity.

13

Calm, sad, secure; with faces worn and mild:
Surely their choice of vigil is the best?
Yea! for our roses fade, the world is wild;
But there, beside the altar, there, is rest.

VILLANELLE OF SUNSET

Come hither, Child! and rest:
This is the end of day,
Behold the weary West!

Sleep rounds with equal zest
Man's toil and children's play:
Come hither, Child! and rest.

My white bird, seek thy nest,
Thy drooping head down lay:
Behold the weary West!

Now are the flowers confest
Of slumber: sleep, as they!
Come hither, Child! and rest.

Now eve is manifest,
And homeward lies our way:
Behold the weary West!

Tired flower! upon my breast,
I would wear thee alway:
Come hither, Child! and rest;
Behold, the weary West!

MY LADY APRIL

Dew on her robe and on her tangled hair;
Twin dewdrops for her eyes; behold her pass,
With dainty step brushing the young, green grass,
The while she trills some high, fantastic air,
Full of all feathered sweetness: she is fair,
And all her flower-like beauty, as a glass,
Mirrors out hope and love: and still, alas!
Traces of tears her languid lashes wear.

Say, doth she weep for very wantonness?
Or is it that she dimly doth foresee
Across her youth the joys grow less and less
The burden of the days that are to be:
Autumn and withered leaves and vanity,
And winter bringing end in barrenness.

TO ONE IN BEDLAM

With delicate, mad hands, behind his sordid bars,
Surely he hath his posies, which they tear and twine;

Those scentless wisps of straw, that miserably line
His strait, caged universe, whereat the dull world stares,
   Pedant and pitiful. O, how his rapt gaze wars
With their stupidity! Know they what dreams divine
Lift his long, laughing reveries like enchaunted wine,
And make his melancholy germane to the stars'?

   O lamentable brother! if those pity thee,
Am I not fain of all thy lone eyes promise me;
Half a fool's kingdom, far from men who sow and reap,
All their days, vanity? Better than mortal flowers,
Thy moon-kissed roses seem: better than love or sleep,
The star-crowned solitude of thine oblivious hours!

AD DOMNULAM SUAM

   Little lady of my heart!
   Just a little longer,
Love me: we will pass and part,
   Ere this love grow stronger.

   I have loved thee, Child! too well,
   To do aught but leave thee:
Nay! my lips should never tell
   Any tale, to grieve thee.

   Little lady of my heart!
   Just a little longer,
I may love thee: we will part,
   Ere my love grow stronger.

   Soon thou leavest fairy-land;
   Darker grow thy tresses:
Soon no more of hand in hand;
   Soon no more caresses!

   Little lady of my heart!
   Just a little longer,
Be a child: then, we will part,
   Ere this love grow stronger.

AMOR UMBRATILIS

   A gift of Silence, sweet!
   Who may not ever hear:
To lay down at your unobservant feet,
   Is all the gift I bear.

   I have no songs to sing,
   That you should heed or know:
I have no lilies, in full hands, to fling
   Across the path you go.

   I cast my flowers away,
   Blossoms unmeet for you!

The garland I have gathered in my day:
  My rosemary and rue.

  I watch you pass and pass,
  Serene and cold: I lay
My lips upon your trodden, daisied grass,
  And turn my life away.

  Yea, for I cast you, sweet!
  This one gift, you shall take:
Like ointment, on your unobservant feet,
  My silence, for your sake.

AMOR PROFANUS

  Beyond the pale of memory,
In some mysterious dusky grove;
A place of shadows utterly,
Where never coos the turtle-dove,
A world forgotten of the sun:
I dreamed we met when day was done,
And marvelled at our ancient love.

  Met there by chance, long kept apart,
We wandered through the darkling glades;
And that old language of the heart
We sought to speak: alas! poor shades!
Over our pallid lips had run
The waters of oblivion,
Which crown all loves of men or maids.

  In vain we stammered: from afar
Our old desire shone cold and dead:
That time was distant as a star,
When eyes were bright and lips were red.
And still we went with downcast eye
And no delight in being nigh,
Poor shadows most uncomforted.

  Ah, Lalage! while life is ours,
Hoard not thy beauty rose and white,
But pluck the pretty, fleeting flowers
That deck our little path of light:
For all too soon we twain shall tread
The bitter pastures of the dead:
Estranged, sad spectres of the night.

VILLANELLE OF MARGUERITE'S

  "A little, *passionately, not at all?*"
  She casts the snowy petals on the air:
And what care we how many petals fall!

Nay, wherefore seek the seasons to forestall?
  It is but playing, and she will not care,
A little, passionately, not at all!

  She would not answer us if we should call
  Across the years: her visions are too fair;
And what care we how many petals fall!

  She knows us not, nor recks if she enthrall
  With voice and eyes and fashion of her hair,
A little, passionately, not at all!

  Knee-deep she goes in meadow grasses tall,
  Kissed by the daisies that her fingers tear:
And what care we how many petals fall!

  We pass and go: but she shall not recall
  What men we were, nor all she made us bear:
"*A little, passionately, not at all!*"
And what care we how many petals fall!

YVONNE OF BRITTANY

  In your mother's apple-orchard,
  Just a year ago, last spring:
Do you remember, Yvonne!
  The dear trees lavishing
Rain of their starry blossoms
  To make you a coronet?
Do you ever remember, Yvonne?
  As I remember yet.

  In your mother's apple-orchard,
  When the world was left behind:
You were shy, so shy, Yvonne!
  But your eyes were calm and kind.
We spoke of the apple harvest,
  When the cider press is set,
And such-like trifles, Yvonne!
  That doubtless you forget.

  In the still, soft Breton twilight,
  We were silent; words were few,
Till your mother came out chiding,
  For the grass was bright with dew:
But I know your heart was beating,
  Like a fluttered, frightened dove.
Do you ever remember, Yvonne?
  That first faint flush of love?

  In the fulness of midsummer,
  When the apple-bloom was shed,
Oh, brave was your surrender,
  Though shy the words you said.
I was glad, so glad, Yvonne!
  To have led you home at last;

Do you ever remember, Yvonne!
  How swiftly the days passed?

YVONNE OF BRITTANY

  In your mother's apple-orchard
  It is grown too dark to stray,
There is none to chide you, Yvonne!
  You are over far away.
There is dew on your grave grass, Yvonne!
  But your feet it shall not wet:
No, you never remember, Yvonne!
  And I shall soon forget.

BENEDICTIO DOMINI

  Without, the sullen noises of the street!
  The voice of London, inarticulate,
Hoarse and blaspheming, surges in to meet
  The silent blessing of the Immaculate.

  Dark is the church, and dim the worshippers,
  Hushed with bowed heads as though by some old spell.
While through the incense-laden air there stirs
  The admonition of a silver bell.

  Dark is the church, save where the altar stands,
  Dressed like a bride, illustrious with light,
Where one old priest exalts with tremulous hands
  The one true solace of man's fallen plight.

  Strange silence here: without, the sounding street
  Heralds the world's swift passage to the fire:
O Benediction, perfect and complete!
  When shall men cease to suffer and desire?

GROWTH

  I watched the glory of her childhood change,
Half-sorrowful to find the child I knew,
  (Loved long ago in lily-time)
Become a maid, mysterious and strange,
  With fair, pure eyes—dear eyes, but not the eyes I knew
  Of old, in the olden time!
  Till on my doubting soul the ancient good
Of her dear childhood in the new disguise
  Dawned, and I hastened to adore
The glory of her waking maidenhood,
  And found the old tenderness within her deepening eyes,
  But kinder than before.

18

AD MANUS PUELLAE

I was always a lover of ladies' hands!
Or ever mine heart came here to tryst,
For the sake of your carved white hands' commands;
The tapering fingers, the dainty wrist;
The hands of a girl were what I kissed.

I remember an hand like a *fleur-de-lys*
When it slid from its silken sheath, her glove;
With its odours passing ambergris:
And that was the empty husk of a love.
Oh, how shall I kiss your hands enough?

They are pale with the pallor of ivories;
But they blush to the tips like a curled sea-shell:
What treasure, in kingly treasuries,
Of gold, and spice for the thurible,
Is sweet as her hands to hoard and tell?

I know not the way from your finger-tips,
Nor how I shall gain the higher lands,
The citadel of your sacred lips:
I am captive still of my pleasant bands,
The hands of a girl, and most your hands.

FLOS LUNAE

I would not alter thy cold eyes,
Nor trouble the calm fount of speech
With aught of passion or surprise.
The heart of thee I cannot reach:
I would not alter thy cold eyes!

I would not alter thy cold eyes;
Nor have thee smile, nor make thee weep:
Though all my life droops down and dies,
Desiring thee, desiring sleep,
I would not alter thy cold eyes.

I would not alter thy cold eyes;
I would not change thee if I might,
To whom my prayers for incense rise,
Daughter of dreams! my moon of night!
I would not alter thy cold eyes.

I would not alter thy cold eyes,
With trouble of the human heart:
Within their glance my spirit lies,
A frozen thing, alone, apart;
I would not alter thy cold eyes.

NON SUM QUALIS ERAM BONAE SUB REGNO CYNARAE

Last night, ah, yesternight, betwixt her lips and mine
There fell thy shadow, Cynara! thy breath was shed
Upon my soul between the kisses and the wine;
And I was desolate and sick of an old passion,
  Yea, I was desolate and bowed my head:
I have been faithful to thee, Cynara! in my fashion.

All night upon mine heart I felt her warm heart beat,
Night-long within mine arms in love and sleep she lay;
Surely the kisses of her bought red mouth were sweet;
But I was desolate and sick of an old passion,
  When I awoke and found the dawn was gray:
I have been faithful to thee, Cynara! in my fashion.

I have forgot much, Cynara! gone with the wind,
Flung roses, roses riotously with the throng,
Dancing, to put thy pale, lost lilies out of mind;
But I was desolate and sick of an old passion,
  Yea, all the time, because the dance was long:
I have been faithful to thee, Cynara! in my fashion.

I cried for madder music and for stronger wine,
But when the feast is finished and the lamps expire,
Then falls thy shadow, Cynara! the night is thine;
And I am desolate and sick of an old passion,
  Yea, hungry for the lips of my desire:
I have been faithful to thee, Cynara! in my fashion.

VANITAS

Beyond the need of weeping,
  Beyond the reach of hands,
May she be quietly sleeping,
  In what dim nebulous lands?
Ah, she who understands!

The long, long winter weather,
  These many years and days,
Since she, and Death, together,
  Left me the wearier ways:
And now, these tardy bays!

The crown and victor's token:
  How are they worth to-day?
The one word left unspoken,
  It were late now to say:
But cast the palm away!

For once, ah once, to meet her,
  Drop laurel from tired hands:
Her cypress were the sweeter,
  In her oblivious lands:
Haply she understands!

Yet, crossed that weary river,
  In some ulterior land,
Or anywhere, or ever,

Will she stretch out a hand?
And will she understand?

EXILE

By the sad waters of separation
Where we have wandered by divers ways,
I have but the shadow and imitation
Of the old memorial days.

In music I have no consolation,
No roses are pale enough for me;
The sound of the waters of separation
Surpasseth roses and melody.

By the sad waters of separation
Dimly I hear from an hidden place
The sigh of mine ancient adoration:
Hardly can I remember your face.

If you be dead, no proclamation
Sprang to me over the waste, gray sea:
Living, the waters of separation
Sever for ever your soul from me.

No man knoweth our desolation;
Memory pales of the old delight;
While the sad waters of separation
Bear us on to the ultimate night.

SPLEEN

I was not sorrowful, I could not weep,
And all my memories were put to sleep.

I watched the river grow more white and strange,
All day till evening I watched it change.

All day till evening I watched the rain
Beat wearily upon the window pane.

I was not sorrowful, but only tired
Of everything that ever I desired.

Her lips, her eyes, all day became to me
The shadow of a shadow utterly.

All day mine hunger for her heart became
Oblivion, until the evening came,

And left me sorrowful, inclined to weep,
With all my memories that could not sleep.

O MORS! QUAM AMARA EST MEMORIA TUA HOMINI PACEM HABENTI IN SUBSTANTIIS SUIS

Exceeding sorrow
Consumeth my sad heart!

Because to-morrow
  We must depart,
Now is exceeding sorrow
  All my part!

  Give over playing,
  Cast thy viol away:
Merely laying
  Thine head my way:
Prithee, give over playing,
  Grave or gay.

  Be no word spoken;
  Weep nothing: let a pale
Silence, unbroken
  Silence prevail!
Prithee, be no word spoken,
  Lest I fail!

  Forget to-morrow!
  Weep nothing: only lay
In silent sorrow
  Thine head my way:
Let us forget to-morrow,
  This one day!

Ah, dans ces mornes séjours
Les jamais sont les toujours
PAUL VERLAINE

You would have understood me, had you waited;
  I could have loved you, dear! as well as he:
Had we not been impatient, dear! and fated
    Always to disagree.

  What is the use of speech? Silence were fitter:
  Lest we should still be wishing things unsaid.
Though all the words we ever spake were bitter,
    Shall I reproach you dead?

  Nay, let this earth, your portion, likewise cover
  All the old anger, setting us apart:
Always, in all, in truth was I your lover;
    Always, I held your heart.

  I have met other women who were tender,
  As you were cold, dear! with a grace as rare.
Think you, I turned to them, or made surrender,
    I who had found you fair?

  Had we been patient, dear! ah, had you waited,
  I had fought death for you, better than he:
But from the very first, dear! we were fated
    Always to disagree.

  Late, late, I come to you, now death discloses
  Love that in life was not to be our part:
On your low lying mound between the roses,
    Sadly I cast my heart.

22

I would not waken you: nay! this is fitter;
  Death and the darkness give you unto me;
Here we who loved so, were so cold and bitter,
    Hardly can disagree.

APRIL LOVE

We have walked in Love's land a little way,
  We have learnt his lesson a little while,
And shall we not part at the end of day,
    With a sigh, a smile?

A little while in the shine of the sun,
  We were twined together, joined lips, forgot
How the shadows fall when the day is done,
    And when Love is not.

We have made no vows—there will none be broke,
  Our love was free as the wind on the hill,
There was no word said we need wish unspoke,
    We have wrought no ill.

So shall we not part at the end of day,
  Who have loved and lingered a little while,
Join lips for the last time, go our way,
    With a sigh, a smile?

VAIN HOPE

Sometimes, to solace my sad heart, I say,
  Though late it be, though lily-time be past,
  Though all the summer skies be overcast,
Haply I will go down to her, some day,
  And cast my rests of life before her feet,
That she may have her will of me, being so sweet
  And none gainsay!

So might she look on me with pitying eyes,
  And lay calm hands of healing on my head:
  "Because of thy long pains be comforted;
For I, even I, am Love: sad soul, arise!"
  So, for her graciousness, I might at last
Gaze on the very face of Love, and hold Him fast
  In no disguise.

Haply, I said, she will take pity on me,
  Though late I come, long after lily-time,
  With burden of waste days and drifted rhyme:
Her kind, calm eyes, down drooping maidenly,
  Shall change, grow soft: there yet is time, meseems,
I said, for solace; though I know these things are dreams
  And may not be!

VAIN RESOLVES

I said: "There is an end of my desire:
  Now have I sown, and I have harvested,
And these are ashes of an ancient fire,
  Which, verily, shall not be quickened.
Now will I take me to a place of peace,
    Forget mine heart's desire;
In solitude and prayer, work out my soul's release.

  "I shall forget her eyes, how cold they were;
  Forget her voice, how soft it was and low,
With all my singing that she did not hear,
  And all my service that she did not know.
I shall not hold the merest memory
    Of any days that were,
Within those solitudes where I will fasten me."

  And once she passed, and once she raised her eyes,
  And smiled for courtesy, and nothing said:
And suddenly the old flame did uprise,
  And all my dead desire was quickened.
Yea! as it hath been, it shall ever be,
    Most passionless, pure eyes!
Which never shall grow soft, nor change, nor pity me.

A REQUIEM

    Neobule, being tired,
Far too tired to laugh or weep,
From the hours, rosy and gray,
Hid her golden face away.
Neobule, fain of sleep,
Slept at last as she desired!

    Neobule! is it well,
That you haunt the hollow lands,
Where the poor, dead people stray,
Ghostly, pitiful and gray,
Plucking, with their spectral hands,
Scentless blooms of asphodel?

    Neobule, tired to death
Of the flowers that I threw
On her flower-like, fair feet,
Sighed for blossoms not so sweet,
Lunar roses pale and blue,
Lilies of the world beneath.

    Neobule! ah, too tired
Of the dreams and days above!
Where the poor, dead people stray,
Ghostly, pitiful and gray,
Out of life and out of love,
Sleeps the sleep which she desired.

BEATA SOLITUDO

24

What land of Silence,
Where pale stars shine
On apple-blossom
And dew-drenched vine,
Is yours and mine?

The silent valley
That we will find,
Where all the voices
Of humankind
Are left behind.

There all forgetting,
Forgotten quite,
We will repose us,
With our delight
Hid out of sight.

The world forsaken,
And out of mind
Honour and labour,
We shall not find
The stars unkind.

And men shall travail,
And laugh and weep;
But we have vistas
Of Gods asleep,
With dreams as deep.

A land of Silence,
Where pale stars shine
On apple-blossoms
And dew-drenched vine,
Be yours and mine!

TERRE PROMISE

Even now the fragrant darkness of her hair
Had brushed my cheek; and once, in passing by,
Her hand upon my hand lay tranquilly:
What things unspoken trembled in the air!

Always I know, how little severs me
From mine heart's country, that is yet so far;
And must I lean and long across a bar,
That half a word would shatter utterly?

Ah might it be, that just by touch of hand,
Or speaking silence, shall the barrier fall;
And she shall pass, with no vain words at all,
But droop into mine arms, and understand!

AUTUMNAL

25

Pale amber sunlight falls across
The reddening October trees,
That hardly sway before a breeze
As soft as summer: summer's loss
Seems little, dear! on days like these.

Let misty autumn be our part!
The twilight of the year is sweet:
Where shadow and the darkness meet
Our love, a twilight of the heart
Eludes a little time's deceit.

Are we not better and at home
In dreamful Autumn, we who deem
No harvest joy is worth a dream?
A little while and night shall come,
A little while, then, let us dream.

Beyond the pearled horizons lie
Winter and night: awaiting these
We garner this poor hour of ease,
Until love turn from us and die
Beneath the drear November trees.

IN TEMPORE SENECTUTIS

When I am old,
And sadly steal apart,
Into the dark and cold,
Friend of my heart!
Remember, if you can,
Not him who lingers, but that other man,
Who loved and sang, and had a beating heart,—
When I am old!

When I am old,
And all Love's ancient fire
Be tremulous and cold:
My soul's desire!
Remember, if you may,
Nothing of you and me but yesterday,
When heart on heart we bid the years conspire
To make us old.

When I am old,
And every star above
Be pitiless and cold:
My life's one love!
Forbid me not to go:
Remember nought of us but long ago,
And not at last, how love and pity strove
When I grew old!

VILLANELLE OF HIS LADY'S TREASURES

26

I took her dainty eyes, as well
As silken tendrils of her hair:
And so I made a Villanelle!

I took her voice, a silver bell,
As clear as song, as soft as prayer;
I took her dainty eyes as well.

It may be, said I, who can tell,
These things shall be my less despair?
And so I made a Villanelle!

I took her whiteness virginal
And from her cheek two roses rare:
I took her dainty eyes as well.

I said: "It may be possible
Her image from my heart to tear!"
And so I made a Villanelle.

I stole her laugh, most musical:
I wrought it in with artful care;
I took her dainty eyes as well;
And so I made a Villanelle.

GRAY NIGHTS

A while we wandered (thus it is I dream!)
Through a long, sandy track of No Man's Land,
Where only poppies grew among the sand,
The which we, plucking, cast with scant esteem,
And ever sadlier, into the sad stream,
Which followed us, as we went, hand in hand,
Under the estranged stars, a road unplanned,
Seeing all things in the shadow of a dream.

And ever sadlier, as the stars expired,
We found the poppies rarer, till thine eyes
Grown all my light, to light me were too tired,
And at their darkening, that no surmise
Might haunt me of the lost days we desired,
After them all I flung those memories!

VESPERAL

Strange grows the river on the sunless evenings!
The river comforts me, grown spectral, vague and dumb:
Long was the day; at last the consoling shadows come:
Sufficient for the day are the day's evil things!

Labour and longing and despair the long day brings;
Patient till evening men watch the sun go west;
Deferred, expected night at last brings sleep and rest:
Sufficient for the day are the day's evil things!

At last the tranquil Angelus of evening rings
Night's curtain down for comfort and oblivion

27

Of all the vanities observèd by the sun:
Sufficient for the day are the day's evil things!

So, some time, when the last of all our evenings
Crowneth memorially the last of all our days,
Not loth to take his poppies man goes down and says,
"Sufficient for the day were the day's evil things!"

THE GARDEN OF SHADOW

Love heeds no more the sighing of the wind
Against the perfect flowers: thy garden's close
Is grown a wilderness, where none shall find
One strayed, last petal of one last year's rose.

O bright, bright hair! O mouth like a ripe fruit!
Can famine be so nigh to harvesting?
Love, that was songful, with a broken lute
In grass of graveyards goeth murmuring.

Let the wind blow against the perfect flowers,
And all thy garden change and glow with spring:
Love is grown blind with no more count of hours
Nor part in seed-tune nor in harvesting.

SOLI CANTARE PERITI ARCADES

Oh, I would live in a dairy,
  And its Colin I would be,
And many a rustic fairy
  Should churn the milk with me.

Or the fields should be my pleasure,
  And my flocks should follow me,
Piping a frolic measure
  For Joan or Marjorie.

For the town is black and weary,
  And I hate the London street;
But the country ways are cheery,
  And country lanes are sweet.

Good luck to you, Paris ladies!
  Ye are over fine and nice
I know where the country maid is,
  Who needs not asking twice.

Ye are brave in your silks and satins,
  As ye mince about the Town;
But her feet go free in pattens,
  If she wear a russet gown.

If she be not queen nor goddess
  She shall milk my brown-eyed herds,
And the breasts beneath her bodice
  Are whiter than her curds.

So I will live in a dairy,
  And its Colin I will be,
And its Joan that I will marry,
  Or, haply, Marjorie.

ON THE BIRTH OF A FRIEND'S CHILD

  Mark the day white, on which the Fates have smiled:
Eugenio and Egeria have a child.
On whom abundant grace kind Jove imparts
If she but copy either parent's parts.
Then, Muses! long devoted to her race,
Grant her Egeria's virtues and her face;
Nor stop your bounty there, but add to it
Eugenio's learning and Eugenio's wit.

EXTREME UNCTION

  Upon the eyes, the lips, the feet,
  On all the passages of sense,
The atoning oil is spread with sweet
  Renewal of lost innocence.

  The feet, that lately ran so fast
  To meet desire, are soothly sealed;
The eyes, that were so often cast
  On vanity, are touched and healed.

  From troublous sights and sounds set free;
  In such a twilight hour of breath,
Shall one retrace his life, or see,
  Through shadows, the true face of death?

  Vials of mercy! Sacring oils!
  I know not where nor when I come,
Nor through what wanderings and toils,
  To crave of you Viaticum.

  Yet, when the walls of flesh grow weak,
  In such an hour, it well may be,
Through mist and darkness, light will break,
  And each anointed sense will see.

AMANTIUM IRAE

  When this, our rose, is faded,
  And these, our days, are done,
In lands profoundly shaded
  From tempest and from sun:
Ah, once more come together,
  Shall we forgive the past,
And safe from worldly weather
  Possess our souls at last?

Or in our place of shadows
 Shall still we stretch an hand
To green, remembered meadows,
 Of that old pleasant land?
And vainly there foregathered,
 Shall we regret the sun?
The rose of love, ungathered?
 The bay, we have not won?

 Ah, child! the world's dark marges
 May lead to Nevermore,
The stately funeral barges
 Sail for an unknown shore,
And love we vow to-morrow,
 And pride we serve to-day:
What if they both should borrow
 Sad hues of yesterday?

 Our pride! Ah, should we miss it,
 Or will it serve at last?
Our anger, if we kiss it,
 Is like a sorrow past.
While roses deck the garden,
 While yet the sun is high,
Doff sorry pride for pardon,
 Or ever love go by.

IMPENITENT ULTIMA

Before my light goes out for ever if God should give me a choice of
 graces,
 I would not reck of length of days, nor crave for things to be;
But cry: "One day of the great lost days, one face of all the faces,
 Grant me to see and touch once more and nothing more to see.

 "For, Lord, I was free of all Thy flowers, but I chose the world's
 sad roses,
 And that is why my feet are torn and mine eyes are blind with sweat,
But at Thy terrible judgment-seat, when this my tired life closes,
 I am ready to reap whereof I sowed, and pay my righteous debt.

 "But once before the sand is run and the silver thread is broken,
 Give me a grace and cast aside the veil of dolorous years,
Grant me one hour of all mine hours, and let me see for a token
 Her pure and pitiful eyes shine out, and bathe her feet with tears."

 Her pitiful hands should calm, and her hair stream down and blind me,
 Out of the sight of night, and out of the reach of fear,
And her eyes should be my light whilst the sun went out behind me,
 And the viols in her voice be the last sound in mine ear.

 Before the ruining waters fall and my life be carried under,
 And Thine anger cleave me through as a child cuts down a flower,
I will praise Thee, Lord in Hell, while my limbs are racked asunder,
 For the last sad sight of her face and the little grace of an hour.

A VALEDICTION

If we must part,
Then let it be like this;
Not heart on heart,
Nor with the useless anguish of a kiss;
But touch mine hand and say:
"*Until to-morrow or some other day,*
If we must part."

Words are so weak
When love hath been so strong:
Let silence speak:
"*Life is a little while, and love is long;*
A time to sow and reap,
And after harvest a long time to sleep.
But words are weak."

SAPIENTIA LUNAE

The wisdom of the world said unto me:
"*Go forth and run, the race is to the brave;*
Perchance some honour tarrieth for thee!"
"As tarrieth," I said, "for sure, the grave."
For I had pondered on a rune of roses,
Which to her votaries the moon discloses.

The wisdom of the world said: "*There are bays:*
Go forth and run, for victory is good,
After the stress of the laborious days."
"Yet," said I, "shall I be the worms' sweet food,"
As I went musing on a rune of roses,
Which in her hour, the pale, soft moon discloses.

Then said my voices: "*Wherefore strive or run,*
On dusty highways ever, a vain race?
The long night cometh, starless, void of sun,
What light shall serve thee like her golden face?"
For I had pondered on a rune of roses,
And knew some secrets which the moon discloses.

"Yea," said I, "for her eyes are pure and sweet
As lilies, and the fragrance of her hair
Is many laurels; and it is not meet
To run for shadows when the prize is here";
And I went reading in that rune of roses
Which to her votaries the moon discloses.

Dum nos fata sinunt, oculos satiemus Amore.—PROPERTIUS

Cease smiling, Dear! a little while be sad,
Here in the silence, under the wan moon;
Sweet are thine eyes, but how can I be glad,
Knowing they change so soon?

For Love's sake, Dear, be silent! Cover me
  In the deep darkness of thy falling hair:
Fear is upon me and the memory
    Of what is all men's share.

  O could this moment be perpetuate!
  Must we grow old, and leaden-eyed and gray,
And taste no more the wild and passionate
    Love sorrows of to-day?

  Grown old, and faded, Sweet! and past desire,
  Let memory die, lest there be too much ruth,
Remembering the old, extinguished fire
    Of our divine, lost youth.

  O red pomegranate of thy perfect mouth!
  My lips' life-fruitage, might I taste and die
Here in thy garden, where the scented south
    Wind chastens agony;

  Reap death from thy live lips in one long kiss,
  And look my last into thine eyes and rest:
What sweets had life to me sweeter than this
    Swift dying on thy breast?

  Or, if that may not be, for Love's sake, Dear!
  Keep silence still, and dream that we shall lie,
Red mouth to mouth, entwined, and always hear
    The south wind's melody,

  Here in thy garden, through the sighing boughs,
  Beyond the reach of time and chance and change,
And bitter life and death, and broken vows,
    That sadden and estrange.

SERAPHITA

  Come not before me now, O visionary face!
Me tempest-tost, and borne along life's passionate sea;
Troublous and dark and stormy though my passage be;
Not here and now may we commingle or embrace,
Lest the loud anguish of the waters should efface
The bright illumination of thy memory,
Which dominates the night; rest, far away from me,
In the serenity of thine abiding place!

  But when the storm is highest, and the thunders blare,
And sea and sky are riven, O moon of all my night!
Stoop down but once in pity of my great despair,
And let thine hand, though over late to help, alight
But once upon my pale eyes and my drowning hair,
Before the great waves conquer in the last vain fight.

EPIGRAM

Because I am idolatrous and have besought,
With grievous supplication and consuming prayer,
The admirable image that my dreams have wrought
Out of her swan's neck and her dark, abundant hair:
The jealous gods, who brook no worship save their own,
Turned my live idol marble and her heart to stone.

QUID NON SUPREMUS, AMANTES?

Why is there in the least touch of her hands
  More grace than other women's lips bestow,
If love is but a slave in fleshly bands
  Of flesh to flesh, wherever love may go?

Why choose vain grief and heavy-hearted hours
  For her lost voice, and dear remembered hair,
If love may cull his honey from all flowers,
  And girls grow thick as violets, everywhere?

Nay! She is gone, and all things fall apart;
  Or she is cold, and vainly have we prayed;
And broken is the summer's splendid heart,
  And hope within a deep, dark grave is laid.

As man aspires and falls, yet a soul springs
  Out of his agony of flesh at last,
So love that flesh enthralls, shall rise on wings
  Soul-centred, when the rule of flesh is past.

Then, most High Love, or wreathed with myrtle sprays,
  Or crownless and forlorn, nor less a star,
Thee may I serve and follow, all my days,
  Whose thorns are sweet as never roses are!

CHANSON SANS PAROLES

In the deep violet air,
  Not a leaf is stirred;
  There is no sound heard,
But afar, the rare
  Trilled voice of a bird.

Is the wood's dim heart,
  And the fragrant pine,
  Incense, and a shrine
Of her coming? Apart,
  I wait for a sign.

What the sudden hush said,
  She will hear, and forsake,
  Swift, for my sake,
Her green, grassy bed:
  She will hear and awake!

She will hearken and glide,
  From her place of deep rest,

33

Dove-eyed, with the breast
Of a dove, to my side:
  The pines bow their crest.

  I wait for a sign:
The leaves to be waved,
The tall tree-tops laved
In a flood of sunshine,
  This world to be saved!

  In the deep violet air,
Not a leaf is stirred;
There is no sound heard,
But afar, the rare
  Trilled voice of a bird.

THE PIERROT OF THE MINUTE

THE CHARACTERS

A MOON MAIDEN PIERROT

THE SCENE

A glade in the Parc due Petit Trianon. In the centre a Doric temple with steps coming down the stage. On the left a little Cupid on a pedestal. Twilight.

[*Pierrot enters with his hands full of lilies. He is burdened with a little basket. He stands gazing at the Temple and the Statue.*]

PIERROT

My journey's end! This surely is the glade
Which I was promised: I have well obeyed!
A clue of lilies was I bid to find,
Where the green alleys most obscurely wind;
Where tall oaks darkliest canopy o'erhead,
And moss and violet make the softest bed;
Where the path ends, and leagues behind me lie
The gleaming courts and gardens of Versailles;
The lilies streamed before me, green and white;
I gathered, following; they led me right,
To the bright temple and the sacred grove:
This is, in truth, the very shrine of Love!

[*He gathers together his flowers and lays them at the foot of Cupid's statue; then he goes timidly up the first steps of the temple and stops.*]

PIERROT

It is so solitary, I grow afraid.
Is there no priest here, no devoted maid?
Is there no oracle, no voice to speak,
Interpreting to me the word I seek?

34

[*A very gentle music of lutes floats out from the temple. Pierrot starts back; he s?*
extreme surprise; then he returns to the foreground, and crouches down in rapt atter?
until the music ceases. His face grows puzzled and petulant.]

PIERROT

Too soon! too soon! in that enchanting strain,
Days yet unlived, I almost lived again:
It almost taught me that I most would know—
Why am I here, and why am I Pierrot?

[*Absently he picks up a lily which has fallen to the ground, and repeats:*]

PIERROT

Why came I here, and why am I Pierrot?
That music and this silence both affright;
Pierrot can never be a friend of night.
I never felt my solitude before—
Once safe at home, I will return no more.
Yet the commandment of the scroll was plain;
While the light lingers let me read again.

[*He takes a scroll from his bosom and reads:*]

PIERROT

"*He loves to-night who never loved before;*
Who ever loved, to-night shall love once more."
I never loved! I know not what love is.
I am so ignorant—but what is this?
[*Reads:*]
"*Who would adventure to encounter Love*
Must rest one night within this hallowed grove.
Cast down thy lilies, which have led thee on,
Before the tender feet of Cupidon."
Thus much is done, the night remains to me.
Well, Cupidon, be my security!
Here is more writing, but too faint to read.
[*He puzzles for a moment, then casts the scroll down.*]

PIERROT

Hence, vain old parchment. I have learnt thy rede!

[*He looks round uneasily, starts at his shadow; then discovers his basket with g?· He*
takes out a flask of wine, pours it into a glass, and drinks.]

PIERROT

Courage, mon Ami! I shall never miss
Society with such a friend as this.
How merrily the rosy bubbles pass,
Across the amber crystal of the glass.
I had forgotten you. Methinks this quest
Can wake no sweeter echo in my breast.

[*Looks round at the statue, and starts.*]

PIERROT

Nay, little god! forgive. I did but jest.

[*He fills another glass, and pours it upon the statue.*]

PIERROT

This libation, Cupid, take,

the lilies at thy feet;
⁓erish Pierrot for their sake:
⁓end him visions strange and sweet,
While he slumbers at thy feet.
Only love kiss him awake!
Only love kiss him awake!

[*Slowly falls the darkness, soft music plays, while Pierrot gathers together fern and foliage into a rough couch at the foot of the steps which lead to the Temple d'Amour. Then he lies down upon it, having made his prayer. It is night.*]

PIERROT [*Softly.*]
Music, more music, far away and faint:
It is an echo of mine heart's complaint.
Why should I be so musical and sad?
I wonder why I used to be so glad?
In single glee I chased blue butterflies,
Half butterfly myself, but not so wise,
For they were twain, and I was only one.
Ah me! how pitiful to be alone.
My brown birds told me much, but in mine ear
They never whispered this—I learned it here:
The soft wood sounds, the rustlings in the breeze,
Are but the stealthy kisses of the trees.
Each flower and fern in this enchanted wood
Leans to her fellow, and is understood;
The eglantine, in loftier station set,
Stoops down to woo the maidly violet.
In gracile pairs the very lilies grow:
None is companionless except Pierrot.
Music, more music! how its echoes steal
Upon my senses with unlocked for weal.
Tired am I, tired, and far from this lone glade
Seems mine old joy in rout and masquerade.
Sleep cometh over me, now will I prove,
ʜ Cupid's grace, what is this thing called love.
[*Sleeps.*]

[*There is more music of lutes for an interval, during which a bright radiance, white and cold, streams from the temple upon the face of Pierrot. Presently a Moon Maiden steps out of the temple; she descends and stands over the sleeper.*]

THE LADY
Who is mortal
Who ve⁓res to-night
To woo a mortal?
Cold, col⁓ moon's light
For sleep a portal,
Bold lover ⁓ght.
Fair is the ⁓,
In soft, silke⁓
Who seeks an ⁓:
Ah, lover of ⁓ial.
Be warned at th⁓
And save thee i⁓

36

[*She stoops over him: Pierrot stirs in his sleep.*]

PIERROT[*Murmuring.*]
Forget not, Cupid. Teach me all thy lore:
"*He loves to-night who never loved before.*"

THE LADY
Unwitting boy! when, be it soon or late,
What Pierrot ever has escaped his fate?
What if I warned him! He might yet evade,
Through the long windings of this verdant glade;
Seek his companions in the blither way,
Which, else, must be as lost as yesterday.
So might he still pass some unheeding hours
In the sweet company of birds and flowers.
How fair he is, with red lips formed for joy,
As softly curved as those of Venus' boy.
Methinks his eyes, beneath their silver sheaves,
Rest tranquilly like lilies under leaves.
Arrayed in innocence, what touch of grace
Reveals the scion of a courtly race?
Well, I will warn him, though, I fear, too late—
What Pierrot ever has escaped his fate?
But, see, he stirs, new knowledge fires his brain,
And Cupid's vision bids him wake again.
Dione's Daughter! but how fair he is,
Would it be wrong to rouse him with a kiss?

[*She stoops down and kisses him, then withdraws into the shadow.*]

PIERROT [*Rubbing his eyes.*]
Celestial messenger! remain, remain;
Or, if a Vision, visit me again!
What is this light, and whither am I come
To sleep beneath the stars so far from home?

[*Rises slowly to his feet.*]

PIERROT
Stay, I remember this is Venus' Grove,
And I am hither come to encounter—

THE LADY [*Coming forward but veiled.*] Love! [*In ecstasy, throwing himself at her feet.*]

PIERROT
Then have I ventured and encountered Love?

THE LADY
Not yet, rash boy! and, if thou wouldst be wise,
Return unknowing; he is safe who flies.

PIERROT
Never, sweet lady, will I leave this place
Until I see the wonder of thy face.
Goddess or Naiad! lady of this Grove,
Made mortal for a night to teach me love,
Unveil thyself, although thy beauty be
Too luminous for my mortality.

THE LADY[*Unveiling.*]
Then, foolish boy, receive at length thy will:
Now knowest thou the greatness of thine ill.

PIERROT
Now have I lost my heart, and gained my goal.

THE LADY Didst thou not read the warning on the scroll? [*Picking up the parchment.*]

PIERROT
I read it all, as on this quest I fared,
Save where it was illegible and hard.

THE LADY
Alack! poor scholar, wast thou never taught
A little knowledge serveth less than naught?
Hadst thou perused—but, stay, I will explain
What was the writing which thou didst disdain.
[*Reads:*]
"*Au Petit Trianon*, at night's full noon,
Mortal, beware the kisses of the moon!
Whoso seeks her she gathers like a flower—
He gives a life, and only gains an hour."

PIERROT[*Laughing recklessly.*]
Bear me away to thine enchanted bower,
All of my life I venture for an hour.

THE LADY
Take up thy destiny of short delight;
I am thy lady for a summer's night.
Lift up your viols, maidens of my train,
And work such havoc on this mortal's brain
That for a moment he may touch and know
Immortal things, and be full Pierrot.
White music, Nymphs! Violet and Eglantine!
To stir his tired veins like magic wine.
What visitants across his spirit glance,
Lying on lilies, while he watch me dance?
Watch, and forget all weary things of earth,
All memories and cares, all joy and mirth,
While my dance woos him, light and rhythmical,
And weaves his heart into my coronal.
Music, more music for his soul's delight:
Love is his lady for a summer's night.

[*Pierrot reclines, and gazes at her while she dances. The dance finished, she beckons to him: he rises dreamily, and stands at her side.*]

PIERROT
Whence came, dear Queen, such magic melody?

THE LADY
Pan made it long ago in Arcady.

PIERROT
I heard it long ago, I know not where,
As I knew thee, or ever I came here.
But I forget all things—my name and race,
All that I ever knew except thy face.

Who art thou, lady? Breathe a name to me,
That I may tell it like a rosary.
Thou, whom I sought, dear Dryad of the trees,
How art thou designate—art thou Heart's-Ease?

THE LADY

Waste not the night in idle questioning,
Since Love departs at dawn's awakening.

PIERROT

Nay, thou art right; what recks thy name or state,
Since thou art lovely and compassionate.
Play out thy will on me: I am thy lyre.

THE LADY

I am to each the face of his desire.

PIERROT

I am not Pierrot, but Venus' dove,
Who craves a refuge on the breast of love.

THE LADY

What wouldst thou of the maiden of the moon?
Until the cock crow I may grant thy boon.

PIERROT

Then, sweet Moon Maiden, in some magic car,
Wrought wondrously of many a homeless star—
Such must attend thy journeys through the skies,—
Drawn by a team of milk-white butterflies,
Whom, with soft voice and music of thy maids,
Thou urgest gently through the heavenly glades;
Mount me beside thee, bear me far away
From the low regions of the solar day;
Over the rainbow, up into the moon,
Where is thy palace and thine opal throne;
There on thy bosom—

THE LADY

Too ambitious boy!
I did but promise thee one hour of joy.
This tour thou plannest, with a heart so light,
Could hardly be completed in a night.
Hast thou no craving less remote than this?

PIERROT

Would it be impudent to beg a kiss?

THE LADY

I say not that: yet prithee have a care!
Often audacity has proved a snare.
How wan and pale do moon-kissed roses grow—
Dost thou not fear my kisses, Pierrot?

PIERROT

As one who faints upon the Libyan plain
Fears the oasis which brings life again!

THE LADY

Where far away green palm trees seem to stand
May be a mirage of the wreathing sand.

39

PIERROT

Nay, dear enchantress, I consider naught,
Save mine own ignorance, which would be taught.

THE LADY

Dost thou persist?

PIERROT

I do entreat this boon!

[*She bends forward, their lips meet: she withdraws with a petulant shiver. She utters a peal of clear laughter.*]

THE LADY

Why art thou pale, fond lover of the moon?

PIERROT

Cold are thy lips, more cold than I can tell
Yet would I hang on them, thine icicle!
Cold is thy kiss, more cold than I could dream
Arctus sits, watching the Boreal stream:
But with its frost such sweetness did conspire
That all my veins are filled with running fire;
Never I knew that life contained such bliss
As the divine completeness of a kiss.

THE LADY

Apt scholar! so love's lesson has been taught,
Warning, as usual, has gone for naught.

PIERROT

Had all my schooling been of this soft kind,
To play the truant I were less inclined.
Teach me again! I am a sorry dunce—
I never knew a task by conning once.

THE LADY

Then come with me! below this pleasant shrine
Of Venus we will presently recline,
Until birds' twitter beckon me away
To mine own home, beyond the milky-way.
I will instruct thee, for I deem as yet
Of Love thou knowest but the alphabet.

PIERROT

In its sweet grammar I shall grow most wise,
If all its rules be written in thine eyes.

[*The lady sits upon a step of the temple. And Pierrot leans upon his elbow at her feet, regarding her.*]

PIERROT

Sweet contemplation! how my senses yearn
To be thy scholar always, always learn.
Hold not so high from me thy radiant mouth,
Fragrant with all the spices of the South;
Nor turn, O sweet! thy golden face away,
For with it goes the light of all my day.
Let me peruse it, till I know by rote
Each line of it, like music, note by note;
Raise thy long lashes, Lady! smile again:

These studies profit me.
[*Taking her hand.*]

THE LADY
Refrain, refrain!

PIERROT[*With passion.*]
I am but studious, so do not stir;
Thou art my star, I thine astronomer!
Geometry was founded on thy lip.
[*Kisses her hand.*]

THE LADY
This attitude becomes not scholarship!
Thy zeal I praise; but, prithee, not so fast,
Nor leave the rudiments until the last.
Science applied is good, but 'twere a schism
To study such before the catechism,
Bear thee more modestly, while I submit
Some easy problems to confirm thy wit.

PIERROT
In all humility my mind I pit
Against her problems which would test my wit.

THE LADY [*Questioning him from a little book bound deliciously in vellum.*]
What is Love?
Is it a folly,
Is it mirth, or melancholy?
Joys above,
Are there many, or not any?
What is love?

PIERROT[*Answering in a very humble attitude of scholarship.*]
If you please,
A most sweet folly!
Full of mirth and melancholy;
Both of these!
In its sadness worth all gladness,
If you please!

THE LADY
Prithee where,
Goes Love a-hiding?
Is he long in his abiding
Anywhere?
Can you bind him when you find him;
Prithee, where?

PIERROT
With spring days
Love comes and dallies:
Upon the mountains, through the valleys
Lie Love's ways.
Then he leaves you and deceives you
In spring days.

THE LADY

Thine answers please me: 'tis thy turn to ask.
To meet thy questioning be now my task.

PIERROT

Since I know thee, dear Immortal,
Is my heart become a blossom,
To be worn upon thy bosom.
When thou turn me from this portal,
Whither shall I, hapless mortal,
Seek love out and win again
Heart of me that thou retain?

THE LADY

In and out the woods and valleys,
Circling, soaring like a swallow,
Love shall flee and thou shalt follow:
Though he stops awhile and dallies,
Never shalt thou stay his malice!
Moon-kissed mortals seek in vain
To possess their hearts again!

PIERROT

Tell me, Lady, shall I never
Rid me of this grievous burden!
Follow Love and find his guerdon
In no maiden whatsoever?
Wilt thou hold my heart for ever?
Rather would I thine forget,
In some earthly Pierrette!

THE LADY

Thus thy fate, whate'er thy will is!
Moon-struck child, go seek my traces
Vainly in all mortal faces!
In and out among the lilies,
Court each rural Amaryllis:
Seek the signet of Love's hand
In each courtly Corisande!

PIERROT

Now, verily, sweet maid, of school I tire:
These answers are not such as I desire.

THE LADY

Why art thou sad?

PIERROT

      I dare not tell.

THE LADY[*Caressingly.*]
          Come, say!

PIERROT

Is love all schooling, with no time to play?

THE LADY

Though all love's lessons be a holiday,
Yet I will humour thee: what wouldst thou play?

PIERROT
What are the games that small moon-maids enjoy.
Or is their time all spent in staid employ?

THE LADY
Sedate they are, yet games they much enjoy:
They skip with stars, the rainbow is their toy.

PIERROT
That is too hard!

THE LADY
       For mortal's play.

PIERROT
           What then?

THE LADY
Teach me some pastime from the world of men.

PIERROT
I have it, maiden.

THE LADY
Can it soon be taught?

PIERROT
A simple game, I learnt it at the Court.
I sit by thee.

THE LADY
     But, prithee, not so near.

PIERROT
That is essential, as will soon appear,
Lay here thine hand, which cold night dews anoint,
Washing its white—

THE LADY
      Now is this to the point?

PIERROT
Prithee, forbear! Such is the game design.

THE LADY
Here is my hand.

PIERROT
     I cover it with mine.

THE LADY
What must I next?

[*They play.*]

PIERROT
     Withdraw.

THE LADY
      It goes too fast.

[*They continue playing, until Pierrot catches her hand.*]

PIERROT[*Laughing.*]
'Tis done. I win my forfeit at the last.

[*He tries to embrace her. She escapes; he chases her round the stage; she eludes him.*]

43

THE LADY
Thou art not quick enough. Who hopes to catch
A moon-beam, must use twice as much despatch.
PIERROT[*Sitting down sulkily.*]
I grow aweary, and my heart is sore,
Thou dost not love me; I will play no more.
[*He buries his face in his hands: the lady stands over him.*]
THE LADY
What is this petulance?
PIERROT
     'Tis quick to tell—
Thou hast but mocked me.
THE LADY
     Nay, I love thee well!
PIERROT
Repeat those words, for still within my breast
A whisper warns me they are said in jest.
THE LADY
I jested not: at daybreak I must go,
Yet loving thee far better than thou know.
PIERROT
Then, by this altar, and this sacred shrine,
Take my sworn troth, and swear thee wholly mine!
The Gods have wedded mortals long ere this.
THE LADY
There was enough betrothal in my kiss.
What need of further oaths?
PIERROT
     That bound not thee!
THE LADY
Peace! since I tell thee that it may not be.
But sit beside me whilst I soothe thy bale
With some moon fancy or celestial tale.
PIERROT
Tell me of thee, and that dim, happy place
Where lies thine home, with maidens of thy race!
THE LADY[*Seating herself.*]
Calm is it yonder, very calm; the air
For mortal's breath is too refined and rare;
Hard by a green lagoon our palace rears
Its dome of agate through a myriad years.
A hundred chambers its bright walls enthrone,
Each one carved strangely from a precious stone.
Within the fairest, clad in purity,
Our mother dwelleth immemorially:
Moon-calm, moon-pale, with moon stones on her gown
The floor she treads with little pearls is sown;
She sits upon a throne of amethysts,
And orders mortal fortunes as she lists;

44

I, and my sisters, all around her stand,
And, when she speaks, accomplish her demand.

PIERROT

Methought grim Clotho and her sisters twain
With shrivelled fingers spun this web of bane!

THE LADY

Theirs and my mother's realm is far apart,
Hers is the lustrous kingdom of the heart,
And dreamers all, and all who sing and love,
Her power acknowledge, and her rule approve.

PIERROT

Me, even me, she hath led into this grove.

THE LADY

Yea, thou art one of hers! But, ere this night,
Often I watched my sisters take their flight
Down heaven's stairway of the clustered stars
To gaze on mortals through their lattice bars;
And some in sleep they woo with dreams of bliss
Too shadowy to tell, and some they kiss.
But all to whom they come, my sisters say,
Forthwith forget all joyance of the day,
Forget their laughter and forget their tears,
And dream away with singing all their years—
Moon-lovers always!

[*She sighs.*]

PIERROT Why art sad, sweet Moon? [*Laughing.*]

THE LADY

For this, my story, grant me now a boon.

PIERROT

I am thy servitor.

THE LADY

        Would, then, I knew
More of the earth, what men and women do.

PIERROT

I will explain.

THE LADY

        Let brevity attend
Thy wit, for night approaches to its end.

PIERROT

Once was I a page at Court, so trust in me:
That's the first lesson of society.

THE LADY

Society?

PIERROT

        I mean the very best
Pardy! thou wouldst not hear about the rest.
I know it not, but am a *petit maître*
At rout and festival and *bal champêtre*

But since example be instruction's ease,
Let's play the thing.—Now, Madame, if you please!

[*He helps her to rise, and leads her forward: then he kisses her hand, bowing over it with a very courtly air.*]

THE LADY
What am I, then?

PIERROT
    A most divine Marquise!
Perhaps that attitude hath too much ease.
[*Passes her.*]Ah, that is better! To complete the plan,
Nothing is necessary save a fan.

THE LADY
Cool is the night, what needs it?

PIERROT
      Madame, pray
Reflect, it is essential to our play.

THE LADY[*Taking a lily.*]
Here is my fan!

PIERROT
    So, use it with intent:
The deadliest arm in beauty's armament!

THE LADY
What do we next?

PIERROT
    We talk!

THE LADY But what about?

PIERROT
We quiz the company and praise the rout;
Are polished, petulant, malicious, sly,
Or what you will, so reputations die.
Observe the Duchess in Venetian lace,
With the red eminence.

THE LADY
    A pretty face!

PIERROT
For something tarter set thy wits to search—
"She loves the churchman better than the church."

THE LADY
Her blush is charming; would it were her own!

PIERROT
Madame is merciless!

THE LADY
    Is that the tone?

PIERROT
The very tone: I swear thou laciest naught.
Madame was evidently bred at Court.

THE LADY
Thou speakest glibly: 'tis not of thine age.

46

PIERROT

I listened much, as best becomes a page.

THE LADY

I like thy Court but little—

PIERROT

              Hush! the Queen!

Bow, but not low—thou knowest what I mean.

THE LADY

Nay, that I know not!

PIERROT

            Though she wear a crown,

'Tis from La Pompadour one fears a frown.

THE LADY

Thou art a child: thy malice is a game.

PIERROT

A most sweet pastime—scandal is its name.

THE LADY

Enough, it wearies me.

PIERROT

           Then, rare Marquise,

Desert the crowd to wander through the trees.

[*He bows low, and she curtsies; they move round the stage. When they pass before the Statue he seizes her hand and falls on his knee.*]

THE LADY

What wouldst thou now?

PIERROT

           Ah, prithee, what, save thee!

THE LADY

Was this included in thy comedy?

PIERROT

Ah, mock me not! In vain with quirk and jest
I strive to quench the passion in my breast;
In vain thy blandishments would make me play:
Still I desire far more than I can say.
My knowledge halts, ah, sweet, be piteous,
Instruct me still, while time remains to us,
Be what thou wist, Goddess, moon-maid, *Marquise,*
So that I gather from thy lips heart's ease,
Nay, I implore thee, think thee how time flies!

THE LADY

Hush! I beseech thee, even now night dies.

PIERROT

Night, day, are one to me for thy soft sake.

[*He entreats her with imploring gestures, she hesitates: then puts her finger on her lip hushing him.*]

THE LADY

It is too late, for hark! the birds awake.

PIERROT

The birds awake! It is the voice of day!

THE LADY

Farewell, dear youth! They summon me away.

[*The light changes, it grows daylights and music imitates the twitter of the birds. They stand gazing at the morning: then Pierrot sinks back upon his bed, he covers his face in his hands.*]

THE LADY[*Bending over him.*]

Music, my maids! His weary senses steep
In soft untroubled and oblivious sleep,
With mandragore anoint his tired eyes,
That they may open on mere memories,
Then shall a vision seem his lost delight,
With love, his lady for a summer's night.
Dream thou hast dreamt all this, when thou awake,
Yet still be sorrowful, for a dream's sake.
I leave thee, sleeper! Yea, I leave thee now,
Yet take my legacy upon thy brow:
Remember me, who was compassionate,
And opened for thee once, the ivory gate.
I come no more, thou shalt not see my face
When I am gone to mine exalted place:
Yet all thy days are mine, dreamer of dreams,
All silvered over with the moon's pale beams:
Go forth and seek in each fair face in vain,
To find the image of thy love again.
All maids are kind to thee, yet never one
Shall hold thy truant heart till day be done.
Whom once the moon has kissed, loves long and late,
Yet never finds the maid to be his mate.
Farewell, dear sleeper, follow out thy fate.

[*The Moon Maiden withdraws: a song is sung from behind: it is full day.*]

THE MOON MAIDEN'S SONG.

Sleep! Cast thy canopy
  Over this sleeper's brain,
Dim grow his memory,
  When he awake again.

  Love stays a summer night,
  Till lights of morning come;
Then takes her wingèd flight
  Back to her starry home.

  Sleep! Yet thy days are mine;
  Love's seal is over thee:
Far though my ways from thine,
  Dim though thy memory.

  Love stays a summer night,
  Till lights of morning come;

48

Then takes her winged flight
  Back to her starry home.
[*When the song is finished, the curtain falls upon Pierrot sleeping.*]
THE END.

DECORATIONS

BEYOND

  Love's aftermath! I think the time is now
That we must gather in, alone, apart
The saddest crop of all the crops that grow,
        Love's aftermath.
Ah, sweet,—sweet yesterday, the tears that start
Can not put back the dial; this is, I trow,
Our harvesting! Thy kisses chill my heart,
Our lips are cold; averted eyes avow
The twilight of poor love: we can but part,
Dumbly and sadly, reaping as we sow,
        Love's aftermath.

DE AMORE

  Shall one be sorrowful because of love,
  Which hath no earthly crown,
  Which lives and dies, unknown?
Because no words of his shall ever move
  Her maiden heart to own
  Him lord and destined master of her own:
Is Love so weak a thing as this,
  Who can not lie awake,
  Solely for his own sake,
For lack of the dear hands to hold, the lips to kiss,
  A mere heart-ache?

  Nay, though love's victories be great and sweet,
  Nor vain and foolish toys,
  His crowned, earthly joys,
Is there no comfort then in love's defeat?
  Because he shall defer,
  For some short span of years all part in her,
  Submitting to forego
  The certain peace which happier lovers know;
Because he shall be utterly disowned,
  Nor length of service bring
  Her least awakening:
Foiled, frustrate and alone, misunderstood, discrowned,
  Is Love less King?

Grows not the world to him a fairer place,
How far soever his days
Pass from his lady's ways,
From mere encounter with her golden face?
Though all his sighing be vain,
Shall he be heavy-hearted and complain?
Is she not still a star,
Deeply to be desired, worshipped afar,
A beacon-light to aid
From bitter-sweet delights, Love's masquerade?
Though he lose many things,
Though much he miss:
The heart upon his heart, the hand that clings,
The memorable first kiss;
Love that is love at all,
Needs not an earthly coronal;
Love is himself his own exceeding great reward,
A mighty lord!

Lord over life and all the ways of breath,
Mighty and strong to save
From the devouring grave;
Yea, whose dominion doth out-tyrant death,
Thou who art life and death in one,
The night, the sun;
Who art, when all things seem:
Foiled, frustrate and forlorn, rejected of to-day
Go with me all my way,
And let me not blaspheme.

THE DEAD CHILD

Sleep on, dear, now
The last sleep and the best,
And on thy brow,
And on thy quiet breast
Violets I throw.

Thy scanty years
Were mine a little while;
Life had no fears
To trouble thy brief smile
With toil or tears.

Lie still, and be
For evermore a child!
Not grudgingly,
Whom life has not defiled,
I render thee.

Slumber so deep,
No man would rashly wake;
I hardly weep,

Fain only, for thy sake.
To share thy sleep.

  Yes, to be dead,
Dead, here with thee to-day,—
When all is said
  'Twere good by thee to lay
My weary head.

  The very best!
  Ah, child so tired of play,
I stand confessed:
  I want to come thy way,
And share thy rest.

CARTHUSIANS

  Through what long heaviness, assayed in what strange fire,
  Have these white monks been brought into the way of peace,
Despising the world's wisdom and the world's desire,
  Which from the body of this death bring no release?

  Within their austere walls no voices penetrate;
  A sacred silence only, as of death, obtains;
Nothing finds entry here of loud or passionate;
  This quiet is the exceeding profit of their pains.

  From many lands they came, in divers fiery ways;
  Each knew at last the vanity of earthly joys;
And one was crowned with thorns, and one was crowned with bays,
  And each was tired at last of the world's foolish noise.

  It was not theirs with Dominic to preach God's holy wrath,
  They were too stern to bear sweet Francis' gentle sway;
Theirs was a higher calling and a steeper path,
  To dwell alone with Christ, to meditate and pray.

  A cloistered company, they are companionless,
  None knoweth here the secret of his brother's heart:
They are but come together for more loneliness,
  Whose bond is solitude and silence all their part.

  O beatific life! Who is there shall gainsay,
  Your great refusal's victory, your little loss,
Deserting vanity for the more perfect way,
  The sweeter service of the most dolorous Cross.

  Ye shall prevail at last! Surely ye shall prevail!
  Your silence and austerity shall win at last:
Desire and mirth, the world's ephemeral lights shall fail,
  The sweet star of your queen is never overcast.

  We fling up flowers and laugh, we laugh across the wine;
  With wine we dull our souls and careful strains of art;
Our cups are polished skulls round which the roses twine:
  None dares to look at Death who leers and lurks apart.

  Move on, white company, whom that has not sufficed!
  Our viols cease, our wine is death, our roses fail:

Pray for our heedlessness, O dwellers with the Christ!
Though the world fall apart, surely ye shall prevail.

THE THREE WITCHES

All the moon-shed nights are over,
And the days of gray and dun;
There is neither may nor clover,
And the day and night are one.

Not an hamlet, not a city
Meets our strained and tearless eyes;
In the plain without a pity,
Where the wan grass droops and dies.

We shall wander through the meaning
Of a day and see no light,
For our lichened arms are leaning
On the ends of endless night.

We, the children of Astarte,
Dear abortions of the moon,
In a gay and silent party,
We are riding to you soon.

Burning ramparts, ever burning!
To the flame which never dies
We are yearning, yearning, yearning,
With our gay and tearless eyes.

In the plain without a pity,
(Not an hamlet, not a city)
Where the wan grass droops and dies.

VILLANELLE OF THE POET'S ROAD

Wine and woman and song,
Three things garnish our way:
Yet is day over long.

Lest we do our youth wrong,
Gather them while we may:
Wine and woman and song.

Three things render us strong,
Vine leaves, kisses and bay;
Yet is day over long.

Unto us they belong,
Us the bitter and gay,
Wine and woman and song.

We, as we pass along,
Are sad that they will not stay;
Yet is day over long.

Fruits and flowers among,
What is better than they:

Wine and woman and song?
Yet is day over long.

VILLANELLE OF ACHERON

By the pale marge of Acheron,
Me thinks we shall pass restfully,
Beyond the scope of any sun.

There all men hie them one by one,
Far from the stress of earth and sea,
By the pale marge of Acheron.

'Tis well when life and love is done,
'Tis very well at last to be,
Beyond the scope of any sun.

No busy voices there shall stun
Our ears: the stream flows silently
By the pale marge of Acheron.

There is the crown of labour won,
The sleep of immortality,
Beyond the scope of any sun.

Life, of thy gifts I will have none,
My queen is that Persephone,
By the pale marge of Acheron,
Beyond the scope of any sun.

SAINT GERMAIN-EN-LAYE

(1887-1895)

Through the green boughs I hardly saw thy face,
They twined so close: the sun was in mine eyes;
And now the sullen trees in sombre lace
Stand bare beneath the sinister, sad skies.

O sun and summer! Say in what far night,
The gold and green, the glory of thine head,
Of bough and branch have fallen? Oh, the white
Gaunt ghosts that flutter where thy feet have sped,

Across the terrace that is desolate,
And rang then with thy laughter, ghost of thee,
That holds its shroud up with most delicate,
Dead fingers, and behind the ghost of me,

Tripping fantastic with a mouth that jeers
At roseal flowers of youth the turbid streams
Toss in derision down the barren years
To death the host of all our golden dreams.

AFTER PAUL VERLAINE

I

Il pleut doucement sur la ville.—RIMBAUD

    Tears fall within mine heart,
As rain upon the town:
Whence does this languor start,
Possessing all mine heart?

    O sweet fall of the rain
Upon the earth and roofs!
Unto an heart in pain,
O music of the rain!

    Tears that have no reason
Fall in my sorry heart:
What! there was no treason?
This grief hath no reason.

    Nay! the more desolate,
Because, I know not why,
(Neither for love nor hate)
Mine heart is desolate.

II

COLLOQUE SENTIMENTAL

    Into the lonely park all frozen fast,
Awhile ago there were two forms who passed.

    Lo, are their lips fallen and their eyes dead,
Hardly shall a man hear the words they said.

    Into the lonely park, all frozen fast,
There came two shadows who recall the past.

    "Dost thou remember our old ecstasy?"—
"Wherefore should I possess that memory?"—

    "Doth thine heart beat at my sole name alway?
Still dost thou see my soul in visions?" "Nay!"—

    "They were fair days of joy unspeakable,
Whereon our lips were joined?"—"I cannot tell."—

    "Were not the heavens blue, was not hope high?"—
"Hope has fled vanquished down the darkling sky."—

    So through the barren oats they wanderèd,
And the night only heard the words they said.

III

SPLEEN

Around were all the roses red,
The ivy all around was black.

Dear, so thou only move thine head,
Shall all mine old despairs awake!

Too blue, too tender was the sky,
The air too soft, too green the sea.

Always I fear, I know not why,
Some lamentable flight from thee.

I am so tired of holly-sprays
And weary of the bright box-tree,

Of all the endless country ways;
Of everything alas! save thee.

IV

The sky is up above the roof
So blue, so soft!
A tree there, up above the roof,
Swayeth aloft.

A bell within that sky we see,
Chimes low and faint:
A bird upon that tree we see,
Maketh complaint.

Dear God! is not the life up there,
Simple and sweet?
How peacefully are borne up there
Sounds of the street!

What hast thou done, who comest
To weep alway?
Where hast thou laid, who comest here,
Thy youth away?

TO HIS MISTRESS

There comes an end to summer,
To spring showers and hoar rime;
His mumming to each mummer
Has somewhere end in time,
And since life ends and laughter,
And leaves fall and tears dry,
Who shall call love immortal,
When all that is must die?

Nay, sweet, let's leave unspoken
The vows the fates gainsay,
For all vows made are broken,
We love but while we may.

55

Let's kiss when kissing pleases,
  And part when kisses pall,
Perchance, this time to-morrow,
  We shall not love at all.

  You ask my love completest,
  As strong next year as now,
The devil take you, sweetest,
  Ere I make aught such vow.
Life is a masque that changes,
  A fig for constancy!
No love at all were better,
  Than love which is not free.

JADIS

  Erewhile, before the world was old,
When violets grew and celandine,
In Cupid's train we were enrolled:
      Erewhile!
Your little hands were clasped in mine,
Your head all ruddy and sun-gold
Lay on my breast which was your shrine,
And all the tale of love was told:
Ah, God, that sweet things should decline,
And fires fade out which were not cold,
      Erewhile.

IN A BRETON CEMETERY

  They sleep well here,
  These fisher-folk who passed their anxious days
  In fierce Atlantic ways;
 And found not there,
  Beneath the long curled wave,
  So quiet a grave.

  And they sleep well
  These peasant-folk, who told their lives away,
  From day to market-day,
 As one should tell,
  With patient industry,
  Some sad old rosary.

  And now night falls,
  Me, tempest-tost, and driven from pillar to post,
  A poor worn ghost,
 This quiet pasture calls;
  And dear dead people with pale hands
  Beckon me to their lands.

TO WILLIAM THEODORE PETERS ON HIS RENAISSANCE CLOAK

56

The cherry-coloured velvet of your cloak
Time hath not soiled: its fair embroideries
Gleam as when centuries ago they spoke
To what bright gallant of Her Daintiness,
Whose slender fingers, long since dust and dead,
For love or courtesy embroidered
The cherry-coloured velvet of this cloak.

Ah! cunning flowers of silk and silver thread,
That mock mortality? the broidering dame,
The page they decked, the kings and courts are dead:
Gone the age beautiful; Lorenzo's name,
The Borgia's pride are but an empty sound;
But lustrous still upon their velvet ground,
Time spares these flowers of silk and silver thread.

Gone is that age of pageant and of pride:
Yet don your cloak, and haply it shall seem,
The curtain of old time is set aside;
As through the sadder coloured throng you gleam;
We see once more fair dame and gallant gay,
The glamour and the grace of yesterday:
The elder, brighter age of pomp and pride.

THE SEA-CHANGE

Where river and ocean meet in a great tempestuous frown,
Beyond the bar, where on the dunes the white-capped rollers break;
Above, one windmill stands forlorn on the arid, grassy down:
I will set my sail on a stormy day and cross the bar and seek
That I have sought and never found, the exquisite one crown,
Which crowns one day with all its calm the passionate and the weak.

When the mad winds are unreined, wilt thou not storm, my sea?
(I have ever loved thee so, I have ever done thee wrong
In drear terrestrial ways.) When I trust myself to thee
With a last great hope, arise and sing thine ultimate, great song
Sung to so many better men, O sing at last to me,
That which when once a man has heard, he heeds not over long.

I will bend my sail when the great day comes; thy kisses on my face
Shall seal all things that are old, outworn; and anger and regret
Shall fade as the dreams and days shall fade, and in thy salt embrace,
When thy fierce caresses blind mine eyes and my limbs grow stark and set,
All that I know in all my mind shall no more have a place:
The weary ways of men and one woman I shall forget.
Point du Pouldu.

DREGS

The fire is out, and spent the warmth thereof
(This is the end of every song man sings!)
The golden wine is drunk, the dregs remain,

Bitter as wormwood and as salt as pain;
And health and hope have gone the way of love
Into the drear oblivion of lost things.
Ghosts go along with us until the end;
This was a mistress, this, perhaps, a friend.
With pale, indifferent eyes, we sit and wait
For the dropt curtain and the closing gate:
This is the end of all the songs man sings.

A SONG

All that a man may pray,
Have I not prayed to thee?
What were praise left to say,
Has not been said by me
  O, ma mie?

Yet thine eyes and thine heart,
Always were dumb to me:
Only to be my part,
Sorrow has come from thee,
  O, ma mie?

Where shall I seek and hide
My grief away with me?
Lest my bitter tears should chide,
Bring brief dismay to thee,
  O, ma mie?

More than a man may pray,
Have I not prayed to thee?
What were praise left to say,
Has not been said by me,
  O, ma mie?

BRETON AFTERNOON

Here, where the breath of the scented-gorse floats through the
  sun-stained air,
On a steep hill-side, on a grassy ledge, I have lain hours long
  and heard
Only the faint breeze pass in a whisper like a prayer,
And the river ripple by and the distant call of a bird.

On the lone hill-side, in the gold sunshine, I will hush me and
  repose,
And the world fades into a dream and a spell is cast on me;
And what was all the strife about, for the myrtle or the rose,
And why have I wept for a white girl's paleness passing ivory!

Out of the tumult of angry tongues, in a land alone, apart,
In a perfumed dream-land set betwixt the bounds of life and death,
Here will I lie while the clouds fly by and delve an hole where my

heart
May sleep deep down with the gorse above and red, red earth beneath.

Sleep and be quiet for an afternoon, till the rose-white angelus
Softly steals my way from the village under the hill:
Mother of God, O Misericord, look down in pity on us,
The weak and blind who stand in our light and wreak ourselves such
*   ill.*

VENITE DESCENDAMUS

Let be at last; give over words and sighing,
  Vainly were all things said:
Better at last to find a place for lying,
  Only dead.

Silence were best, with songs and sighing over;
  Now be the music mute;
Now let the dead, red leaves of autumn cover
  A vain lute.

Silence is best: for ever and for ever,
  We will go down and sleep,
Somewhere beyond her ken, where she need never
  Come to weep.

Let be at last: colder she grows and colder;
  Sleep and the night were best;
Lying at last where we cannot behold her,
  We may rest.

TRANSITION

A little while to walk with thee, dear child;
  To lean on thee my weak and weary head;
Then evening comes: the winter sky is wild,
  The leafless trees are black, the leaves long dead.

A little while to hold thee and to stand,
  By harvest-fields of bending golden corn;
Then the predestined silence, and thine hand,
  Lost in the night, long and weary and forlorn.

A little while to love thee, scarcely time
  To love thee well enough; then time to part,
To fare through wintry fields alone and climb
  The frozen hills, not knowing where thou art.

Short summer-time and then, my heart's desire,
  The winter and the darkness: one by one
The roses fall, the pale roses expire
  Beneath the slow decadence of the sun.

EXCHANGES

59

All that I had I brought,
  Little enough I know;
A poor rhyme roughly wrought,
  A rose to match thy snow:
All that I had I brought.

  Little enough I sought:
  But a word compassionate,
A passing glance, or thought,
  For me outside the gate:
Little enough I sought.

  Little enough I found:
  All that you had, perchance!
With the dead leaves on the ground,
  I dance the devil's dance.
All that you had I found.

TO A LADY ASKING FOOLISH QUESTIONS

  Why am I sorry, Chloe? Because the moon is far:
And who am I to be straitened in a little earthly star?

  Because thy face is fair? And what if it had not been,
The fairest face of all is the face I have not seen.

  Because the land is cold, and however I scheme and plot,
I cannot find a ferry to the land where I am not.

  Because thy lips are red and thy breasts upbraid the snow?
(There is neither white nor red in the pleasance where I go.)

  Because thy lips grow pale and thy breasts grow dun and fall?
I go where the wind blows, Chloe, and am not sorry at all.

RONDEAU

  Ah, Manon, say, why is it we
Are one and all so fain of thee?
Thy rich red beauty debonnaire
In very truth is not more fair,
Than the shy grace and purity
That clothe the maiden maidenly;
Her gray eyes shine more tenderly
And not less bright than thine her hair;
  Ah, Manon, say!
Expound, I pray, the mystery
Why wine-stained lip and languid eye,
And most unsaintly Maenad air,
Should move us more than all the rare
White roses of virginity?
  Ah, Manon, say!

MORITURA

A song of the setting sun!
The sky in the west is red,
And the day is all but done:
  While yonder up overhead,
    All too soon,
There rises, so cold, the cynic moon.

  A song of a winter day!
  The wind of the north doth blow,
From a sky that's chill and gray,
  On fields where no crops now grow,
    Fields long shorn
Of bearded barley and golden corn.

  A song of an old, old man!
  His hairs are white and his gaze,
Long bleared in his visage wan,
  With its weight of yesterdays,
    Joylessly
He stands and mumbles and looks at me,

  A song of a faded flower!
  'Twas plucked in the tender bud,
And fair and fresh for an hour,
  In a lady's hair it stood.
    Now, ah, now,
Faded it lies in the dust and low.

LIBERA ME

  Goddess the laughter-loving, Aphrodite, befriend!
Long have I served thine altars, serve me now at the end,
Let me have peace of thee, truce of thee, golden one, send.

  Heart of my heart have I offered thee, pain of my pain,
Yielding my life for the love of thee into thy chain;
Lady and goddess be merciful, loose me again.

  All things I had that were fairest, my dearest and best,
Fed the fierce flames on thine altar: ah, surely, my breast
Shrined thee alone among goddesses, spurning the rest.

  Blossom of youth thou hast plucked of me, flower of my days;
Stinted I nought in thine honouring, walked in thy ways,
Song of my soul pouring out to thee, all in thy praise.

  Fierce was the flame while it lasted, and strong was thy wine,
Meet for immortals that die not, for throats such as thine,
Too fierce for bodies of mortals, too potent for mine.

  Blossom and bloom hast thou taken, now render to me
Ashes of life that remain to me, few though they be,
Truce of the love of thee, Cyprian, let me go free.

  Goddess the laughter-loving, Aphrodite, restore
Life to the limbs of me, liberty, hold me no more
Having the first-fruits and flower of me, cast me the core.

TO A LOST LOVE

I seek no more to bridge the gulf that lies
Betwixt our separate ways;
For vainly my heart prays,
Hope droops her head and dies;
I see the sad, tired answer in your eyes.

I did not heed, and yet the stars were clear;
Dreaming that love could mate
Lives grown so separate;—
But at the best, my dear,
I see we should not have been very near.

I knew the end before the end was nigh:
The stars have grown so plain;
Vainly I sigh, in vain
For things that come to some,
But unto you and me will never come.

WISDOM

Love wine and beauty and the spring,
While wine is red and spring is here,
And through the almond blossoms ring
The dove-like voices of thy Dear.

Love wine and spring and beauty while
The wine hath flavour and spring masks
Her treachery in so soft a smile
That none may think of toil and tasks.

But when spring goes on hurrying feet,
Look not thy sorrow in the eyes,
And bless thy freedom from thy sweet:
This is the wisdom of the wise.

IN SPRING

See how the trees and the osiers lithe
Are green bedecked and the woods are blithe,
The meadows have donned their cape of flowers,
The air is soft with the sweet May showers,
And the birds make melody:
But the spring of the soul, the spring of the soul,
Cometh no more for you or for me.

The lazy hum of the busy bees
Murmureth through the almond trees;
The jonquil flaunteth a gay, blonde head,
The primrose peeps from a mossy bed,
And the violets scent the lane.
But the flowers of the soul, the flowers of the soul,
For you and for me bloom never again.

A LAST WORD

Let us go hence: the night is now at hand;
  The day is overworn, the birds all flown;
  And we have reaped the crops the gods have sown
Despair and death; deep darkness o'er the land,
Broods like an owl; we cannot understand
  Laughter or tears, for we have only known
  Surpassing vanity: vain things alone
Have driven our perverse and aimless band.

  Let us go hence, somewhither strange and cold,
  To Hollow Lands where just men and unjust
  Find end of labour, where's rest for the old,
Freedom to all from love and fear and lust.
Twine our torn hands! O pray the earth enfold
Our life-sick hearts and turn them into dust.

DILEMMAS

STORIES AND STUDIES IN SENTIMENT

First Published in Book Form in 1895

THE DIARY OF A SUCCESSFUL MAN

1st October, 188— Hotel du Lys, Bruges.

After all, few places appeal to my imagination more potently than this autumnal old city—the most mediæval town in Europe. I am glad that I have come back here at last. It is melancholy indeed, but then at my age one's pleasures are chiefly melancholy. One is essentially of the autumn, and it is always autumn at Bruges. I thought I had been given back my youth when I awoke this morning and heard the Carillon, chiming out, as it has done, no doubt, intermittently, since I heard it last—twenty years ago. Yes, for a moment, I thought I was young again—only for a moment. When I went out into the streets and resumed acquaintance with all my old haunts, the illusion had gone. I strolled into Saint Sauveur's, wandered a while through its dim, dusky aisles, and then sat down near the high altar, where the air was heaviest with stale incense, and indulged in retrospect. I was there for more than an hour. I doubt whether it was quite wise. At my time of life one had best keep out of cathedrals; they are vault-like places, pregnant with rheumatism—at best they are full of ghosts. And a good many *revenants* visited me during that hour of meditation. Afterwards I paid a visit to the Memlings in the Hôpital. Nothing has altered very much; even the women, with their placid, ugly Flemish faces, sitting eternally in their doorways with the eternal lace-pillow, might be the same women. In the afternoon I went to the Béguinage, and sat there long in the shadow of a tree, which must have grown up since my time, I think. I sat there too long, I fear, until the dusk and the chill drove me home to dinner. On the whole perhaps it was a mistake to come back. The sameness of this terribly constant old city seems to intensify the change that has come to oneself. Perhaps if I had come back with Lorimer I should have noticed it less. For, after all, the years have been kind to me, on the whole; they have given me most things which I set my heart upon, and if they had not broken a most perfect friendship, I would forgive them the rest. I sometimes feel, however, that one sacrifices too much to one's success. To slave twenty years at the Indian bar has its drawbacks, even when it does leave one at fifty, prosperous *à mourir d'ennui*. Yes, I must admit that I am prosperous, disgustingly prosperous, and—my wife is dead, and Lorimer—Lorimer has altogether passed out of my life. Ah, it is a mistake to keep a journal—a mistake.

3rd October.

I vowed yesterday that I would pack my portmanteau and move on to Brussels, but to-day finds me still at Bruges. The charm of the old Flemish city grows on me. To-day I carried my peregrinations further a-field. I wandered about the Quais and stood on the old bridge where one obtains such a perfect glimpse, through a trellis of chestnuts, of the red roof and spires of Notre Dame. But the particular locality matters nothing; every nook and corner of Bruges teems with reminiscences. And how fresh they are! At Bombay I had not time to remember or to regret; but to-day the whole dead and forgotten story rises up like a ghost to haunt me. At times, moreover, I have a curious, fantastic feeling, that some day or other, in some mildewing church, I shall come face to face with Lorimer. He was older than I, he must be greatly altered, but I should know him. It is strange how intensely I desire to meet him. I suppose it is chiefly curiosity. I should like to feel sure of him, to explain his silence. He cannot be dead. I am told that he had pictures in this last Academy—and yet, never to have written—never once, through all these years. I suppose there are few friendships which can stand the test of correspondence. Still it is inexplicable, it is not like Lorimer. He could not have harboured a grudge against me— for what? A boyish infatuation for a woman who adored him, and whom he adored. The idea is preposterous, they must have laughed over my folly often, of winter evenings by their fireside. For they married, they must have married, they were made for each other and they knew it. Was their marriage happy I wonder? Was it as successful as mine, though perhaps a little less commonplace? It is strange, though, that I never heard of it, that he never wrote to me once, not through all those years.

4th October.

Inexplicable! Inexplicable! *Did* they marry after all? Could there have been some gigantic misunderstanding? I paid a pilgrimage this morning which hitherto I had deferred, I know not precisely why. I went to the old house in the Rue d'Alva—where she lived, our Comtesse. And the sight of its grim, historic frontal made twenty years seem as yesterday. I meant to content myself with a mere glimpse at the barred windows, but the impulse seized me to ring the bell which I used to ring so often. It was a foolish, fantastic impulse, but I obeyed it. I found it was occupied by an Englishman, a Mr. Venables— there seem to be more English here than in my time—and I sent in my card and asked if I might see the famous dining-room. There was no objection raised, my host was most courteous, my name, he said, was familiar to him; he is evidently proud of his dilapidated old palace, and has had the grace to save it from the attentions of the upholsterer. No! twenty years have produced very little change in the room where we had so many pleasant sittings. The ancient stamped leather on the walls is perhaps a trifle more ragged, the old oak panels not blacker—that were impossible—but a trifle more worm-eaten; it is the same room. I must have seemed a sad boor to my polite cicerone as I stood, hat in hand, and silently took in all the old familiar details. The same smell of mildewed antiquity, I could almost believe the same furniture. And indeed my host tells me that he took over the house as it was, and that some of the chairs and tables are scarcely more youthful than the walls. Yes, there by the huge fireplace was the same quaintly carved chair where she always sat. Ah, those delicious evenings when one was five-and-twenty. For the moment I should not have been surprised if she had suddenly taken shape before my eyes, in the old seat, the slim, girlish woman in her white dress, her hands folded in her lap, her quiet eyes gazing dreamily into the red fire, a subtle air of distinction in her whole posture.... She would be old now, I suppose. Would she? Ah no, she was not one of the women who grow old.... I caught up the thread of my host's discourse just as he was pointing it with a sharp rap upon one of the most time-stained panels.

'Behind there,' he remarked, with pardonable pride, 'is the secret passage where the Duc d'Alva was assassinated.'

I smiled apologetically.

'Yes,' I said, 'I know it. I should explain perhaps—my excuse for troubling you was not merely historic curiosity. I have more personal associations with this room. I spent some charming hours in it a great many years ago-' and for the moment I had forgotten that I was nearly fifty.

'Ah,' he said, with interest, 'you know the late people, the Fontaines.'

'No,' I said, 'I am afraid I have never heard of them. I am very ancient.
In my time it belonged to the Savaresse family.'

'So I have heard,' he said, 'but that was long ago. I have only had it a few years.
Fontaine my landlord bought it from them. Did you know M. le Comte!'

'No,' I answered, 'Madame la Comtesse. She was left a widow very shortly after her marriage. I never knew M. le Comte.'

My host shrugged his shoulders.

'From all accounts,' he said, 'you did not lose very much.'

'It was an unhappy marriage,' I remarked, vaguely, 'most unhappy. Her second marriage promised greater felicity.'

Mr. Venables looked at me curiously.

'I understood,' he began, but he broke off abruptly. 'I did not know Madame de Savaresse married again.'

His tone had suddenly changed, it had grown less cordial, and we parted shortly afterwards with a certain constraint. And as I walked home pensively curious, his interrupted sentence puzzled me. Does he look upon me as an impostor, a vulgar gossip-monger? What has he heard, what does he know of her? Does he know anything? I cannot help believing so. I almost wish I had asked him definitely, but he would have misunderstood my motives. Yet, even so, I wish I had asked him.

6th October.

I am still living constantly in the past, and the fantastic feeling, whenever I enter a church or turn a corner that I shall meet Lorimer again, has grown into a settled conviction. Yes, I shall meet him, and in Bruges.... It is strange how an episode which one has thrust away out of sight and forgotten for years will be started back into renewed life by the merest trifle. And for the last week it has all been as vivid as if it happened yesterday. To-night I have been putting questions to myself—so far with no very satisfactory answer. *Was* it a boyish infatuation after all? Has it passed away as utterly as I believed? I can see her face now as I sit by the fire with the finest precision of detail. I can hear her voice, that soft, low voice, which was none the less sweet for its modulation of sadness. I think there are no women like her now-a-days—none, none! *Did* she marry Lorimer? and if not—? It seems strange now that we should have both been so attracted, and yet not strange when one considers it. At least we were never jealous of one another. How the details rush back upon one! I think we must have fallen in love with her at the same moment—for we were together when we saw her for the first time, we were together when we went first to call on her in the Rue d'Alva—I doubt if we ever saw her except together. It was soon after we began to get intimate that she wore white again. She told us that we had given her back her youth. She joined our sketching expeditions with the most supreme contempt for *les convenances*; when she was not fluttering round, passing from Lorimer's canvas to mine with her sweetly inconsequent criticism, she sat in the long grass and read to us—André Chénier and Lamartine. In the evening we went to see her; she denied herself to the rest of the world, and we sat for hours in that ancient room in the delicious twilight, while she sang to us—she sang divinely—little French *chansons*, gay and sad, and snatches of *operette*. How we adored her! I think she knew from the first how it would be and postponed it as long as she could. But at last she saw that it was inevitable…. I remember the last evening that we were there—remember— shall I ever forget it? We had stayed beyond our usual hour and when we rose to go we all of us knew that those pleasant irresponsible evenings had come to an end. And both Lorimer and I stood for a moment on the threshold before we said good-night, feeling I suppose that one of us was there for the last time.

And how graceful, how gracious she was as she held out one little white hand to Lorimer and one to me. 'Good-night, dear friends,' she said, 'I like you both so much—so much. Believe me, I am grateful to you both—for having given me back my faith in life, in friendship, believe that, will you not, *mes amis*?' Then for just one delirious moment her eyes met mine and it seemed to me—ah, well, after all it was Lorimer she loved.

7th October.

It seems a Quixotic piece of folly now, our proposal we would neither take advantage of the other, but we both of us *must* speak. We wrote to her at the same time and likely enough, in the same words, we posted our letters by the same post. To-day I had the curiosity to take out her answer to me from my desk, and I read it quite calmly and dispassionately, the poor yellow letter with the faded ink, which wrote 'Finis' to my youth and made a man of me.

'*Pauvre cher Ami,*' she wrote to me, and when I had read that, for the first time in my life and the only time Lorimer's superiority was bitter to me. The rest I deciphered through scalding tears.

'*Pauvre cher Ami*, I am very sorry for you, and yet I think you should have guessed and have spared yourself this pain, and me too a little. No, my friend, that which you ask of me is impossible. You are my dear friend, but it is your brother whom I love—your brother, for are you not as brothers, and I cannot break your beautiful friendship. No, that must not be. See, I ask one favour of you—I have written also to him, only one little word "Viens,"—but will you not go to him and tell him for me? Ah, my brother, my heart bleeds for you. I too have suffered in my time. You will go away now, yes, that is best, but you will return when this fancy of yours has passed. Ah forgive me—that I am happy—forgive us, forgive me. Let us still be friends. Adieu! Au revoir.

'Thy Sister,
DELPHINE.'

I suppose it was about an hour later that I took out my letter to Lorimer. I told him as I told myself, that it was the fortune of war, that she had chosen the better man, but I could not bear to stay and see their happiness. I was in London before the evening. I wanted work, hard, grinding work, I was tired of being a briefless barrister, and as it happened, an Indian opening offered itself at the very moment when I had decided that Europe had become impossible to me. I accepted it, and so those two happy ones passed out of my life.

Twenty years ago! and in spite of his promise he has never written from that day till this, not so much as a line to tell me of his marriage. I made a vow then that I would get over my folly, and it seemed to me that my vow was kept. And yet here to-day, in Bruges, I am asking myself whether after all it has been such a great success, whether sooner or later one does not have to pay for having been hard and strong, for refusing to suffer.... I must leave this place, it is too full of Madame de Savaresse.... Is it curiosity which is torturing me? I *must* find Lorimer. If he married her, why has he been so persistently silent? If he did not marry her, what in Heaven's name does it mean? These are vexing questions.

10th October.

In the Church of the Dames Rouges, I met to-day my old friend Sebastian Lorimer. Strange! Strange! He was greatly altered, I wonder almost that I recognised him. I had strolled into the church for benediction, for the first time since I have been back here, and when the service was over and I swung back the heavy door, with the exquisite music of the 'O Salutaris,' sung by those buried women behind the screen still echoing in my ear, I paused a moment to let a man pass by me. It was Lorimer, he looked wild and worn; it was no more than the ghost of my old friend. I was shocked and startled by his manner. We shook hands quite impassively as if we had parted yesterday. He talked in a rambling way as we walked towards my hotel, of the singing of the nuns, of the numerous religious processions, of the blessed doctrine of the intercession of saints. The old melodious voice was unchanged, but it was pitched in the singularly low key which I have noticed some foreign priests acquire who live much in churches. I gather that he has become a Catholic. I do not know what intangible instinct, or it may be fear, prevented me from putting to him the vital question which has so perplexed me. It is astonishing how his face has changed, what an extraordinary restlessness his speech and eye have acquired. It never was so of old. My first impression was that he was suffering from some acute form of nervous disorder, but before I left him a more unpleasant suspicion was gradually forced upon me. I cannot help thinking that there is more than a touch of insanity in my old friend. I tried from time to time to bring him down to personal topics, but he eluded them dexterously, and it was only for a moment or so that I could keep him away from the all absorbing subject of the Catholic Church, which seems in some of its more sombre aspects to exercise an extraordinary fascination over him. I asked him if he often visited Bruges.

He looked up at me with a curious expression of surprise.

'I live here,' he said, 'almost always.' I have done so for years....' Presently he added hurriedly, 'You have come back. I thought you would come back, but you have been gone a long time—oh, a long time! It seems years since we met. Do you remember—?' He checked himself; then he added in a low whisper, 'We all come back, we all come back.'

He uttered a quaint, short laugh.

'One can be near—very near, even if one can never be quite close.'

He tells me that he still paints, and that the Academy, to which he sends a picture yearly, has recently elected him an Associate. But his art does not seem to absorb him as it did of old, and he speaks of his success drily and as a matter of very secondary importance. He refused to dine with me, alleging an engagement, but that so hesitatingly and with such vagueness that I could perceive it was the merest pretext. His manner was so strange and remote that I did not venture to press him. I think he is unhappily conscious of his own frequent incoherencies and at moments there are quite painful pauses when he is obviously struggling with dumb piteousness to be lucid, to collect himself and pick up certain lost threads in his memory. He is coming to see me this evening, at his own suggestion, and I am waiting for him now with a strange terror oppressing me. I cannot help thinking that he possesses the key to all that has so puzzled me, and that to-night he will endeavour to speak.

11th October.

Poor Lorimer! I have hardly yet got over the shock which his visit last night caused me, and the amazement with which I heard and read between the lines of his strange confession. His once clear reason is, I fear, hopelessly obscured, and how much of his story is hallucination, I cannot say. His notions of time and place are quite confused, and out of his rambling statement I can only be sure of one fact. It seems that he has done me a great wrong, an irreparable wrong, which he has since bitterly repented.

And in the light of this poor wretch's story, a great misunderstanding is rolled away, and I am left with the conviction that the last twenty years have been after all a huge blunder, an irrevocable and miserable mistake. Through my own rash precipitancy and Lorimer's weak treachery, a trivial mischance that a single word would have rectified, has been prolonged beyond hope of redress. It seems that after all it was not Lorimer whom she chose. Madame de Savaresse writing to us both twenty years ago, made a vital and yet not inexplicable mistake. She confused her envelopes, and the letter which I received was never meant for me, although it was couched in such ambiguous terms that until to-day the possibility of this error never dawned on me. And my letter, the one little word of which she spoke, was sent to Lorimer. Poor wretch! he did me a vital injury—yes, I can say that now—a vital injury, but on the whole I pity him. To have been suddenly dashed down from the pinnacles of happiness, it must have been a cruel blow. He tells me that when he saw her that afternoon and found out his mistake, he had no thought except to recall me. He actually came to London for that purpose, vowed to her solemnly that he would bring me back; it was only in England, that, to use his own distraught phrase, the Devil entered into possession of him. His half-insane ramblings gave me a very vivid idea of that fortnight during which he lay hid in London, trembling like a guilty thing, fearful at every moment that he might run across me and yet half longing for the meeting with the irresoluteness of the weak nature, which can conceive and to a certain extent execute a *lâcheté*, yet which would always gladly yield to circumstance and let chance or fate decide the issue. And to the very last Lorimer was wavering—had almost sought me out, and thrown himself on my mercy, when the news came that I had sailed.

Destiny who has no weak scruples, had stepped in and sealed Delphine's mistake for all time, after her grim fashion. When he went back to Bruges, and saw Madame de Savaresse, I think she must have partly guessed his baseness. Lorimer was not strong enough to be a successful hypocrite, and that meeting, I gather, was also their final parting. She must have said things to him in her beautiful quiet voice which he has never forgotten. He went away and each day he was going to write to me, and each day he deferred it, and then he took up the *Times* one morning and read the announcement of my marriage. After that it seemed to him that he could only be silent....

Did *she* know of it too? Did she suffer or did she understand? Poor woman! poor woman! I wonder if she consoled herself, as I did, and if so how she looks back on her success? I wonder whether she is happy, whether she is dead? I suppose these are questions which will remain unanswered. And yet when Lorimer left me at a late hour last night, it seemed to me that the air was full of unspoken words. Does he know anything of her now! I have a right to ask him these things. And to-morrow I am to meet him, he made the request most strangely—at the same place where we fell in with each other to-day—until to-morrow then!

12th October.

I have just left Sebastian Lorimer at the Church of the Dames Rouges. I hope I was not cruel, but there are some things which one can neither forget nor forgive, and it seemed to me that when I knew the full measure of the ruin he had wrought, my pity for him withered away. 'I hope, Lorimer,' I said, 'that we may never meet again.' And, honestly, I cannot forgive him. If she had been happy, if she had let time deal gently with her—ah yes, even if she were dead—it might be easier. But that this living entombment, this hopeless death in life should befall her, she so magnificently fitted for life's finer offices, ah, the pity of it, the pity of it!... But let me set down the whole sad story as it dawned

68

upon me this afternoon in that unearthly church. I was later than the hour appointed; vespers were over and a server, taper in hand, was gradually transforming the gloom of the high altar into a blaze of light. With a strange sense of completion I took my place next to the chair by which Lorimer, with bowed head, was kneeling, his eyes fixed with a strange intentness on the screen which separated the outer worshippers from the chapel or gallery which was set apart for the nuns. His lips moved from time to time spasmodically, in prayer or ejaculation: then as the jubilant organ burst out, and the officiating priest in his dalmatic of cloth of gold passed from the sacristy and genuflected at the altar, he seemed to be listening in a very passion of attention. But as the incense began to fill the air, and the Litany of Loreto smote on my ear to some sorrowful, undulating Gregorian, I lost thought of the wretched man beside me; I forgot the miserable mistake that he had perpetuated, and I was once more back in the past—with Delphine—kneeling by her side. Strophe by strophe that perfect litany rose and was lost in a cloud of incense, in the mazy arches of the roof.

'Janua coeli,
Stella matutina,
Salus infirmorum, Ora pro nobis!'

In strophe and antistrophe: the melancholy, nasal intonation of the priest died away, and the exquisite women's voices in the gallery took it up with exultation, and yet with something like a sob—a sob of limitation.

'Refugium peccatorum,
Consolatrix afflictorum,
Auxilium Christianorum, Ora pro nobis!'

And so on through all the exquisite changes of the hymn, until the time of the music changed, and the priest intoned the closing line.

'Ora pro nobis, Sancta Dei Genetrix!'

and the voices in the gallery answered:

'Ut digni efficiamur promissionibus Christi.'

There was one voice which rose above all the others, a voice of marvellous sweetness and power, which from the first moment had caused me a curious thrill. And presently Lorimer bent down and whispered to me: 'So near,' he murmured, 'and yet so far away—so near, and yet never quite close!'

But before he had spoken I had read in his rigid face, in his eyes fixed with such a passion of regret on the screen, why we were there—whose voice it was we had listened to.

I rose and went out of the church quietly and hastily; I felt that to stay there one moment longer would be suffocation…. Poor woman! so this is how she sought consolation, in religion! Well, there are different ways for different persons—and for me—what is there left for me? Oh, many things, no doubt, many things. Still, for once and for the last time, let me set myself down as a dreary fraud. I never forgot her, not for one hour or day, not even when it seemed to me that I had forgotten her most, not even when I married. No woman ever represented to me the same idea as Madame de Savaresse. No woman's voice was ever sweet to me after hers, the touch of no woman's hand ever made my heart beat one moment quicker for pleasure or for pain, since I pressed hers for the last time on that fateful evening twenty years ago. Even so—!…

When the service was over and the people had streamed out and dispersed, I went back for the last time into the quiet church. A white robed server was extinguishing the last candle on the altar; only the one red light perpetually vigilant before the sanctuary, made more visible the deep shadows everywhere.

Lorimer was still kneeling with bowed head in his place. Presently he rose and came towards me. 'She was there—Delphine—you heard her. Ah, Dion, she loves you, she always loves you, you are avenged.'

I gather that for years he has spent hours daily in this church, to be near her, and hear her voice, the magnificent voice rising above all the other voices in the chants of her religion. But he will never see her, for is she not of the Dames Rouges! And I remember now all the stories of the Order, of its strictness, its austerity, its perfect isolation. And chiefly, I remember how they say that only twice after one of these nuns has taken her vows is she seen of any one except those of her community; once, when she enters the Order, the door of the convent is thrown back and she is seen for a single moment in the scarlet habit of the Order, by the world, by all who care to gaze; and once more, at the last, when clad in the same coarse red garb, they bear her out quietly, in her coffin, into the church.

And of this last meeting, Lorimer, I gather, is always restlessly expectant, his whole life concentrated, as it were, in a very passion of waiting for a moment which will surely come. His theory, I confess, escapes me, nor can I guess how far a certain feverish remorse, an intention of expiation may be set as a guiding spring in his unhinged mind, and account, at least in part, for the fantastic attitude which he must have adopted for many years. If I cannot forgive him, at least I bear him no malice, and for the rest, our paths will hardly cross again. One takes up one's life and expiates its errors, each after one's several fashion—and my way is not Lorimer's. And now that it is all so clear, there is nothing to keep me here any longer, nothing to bring me back again. For it seemed to me to-day, strangely enough, as though a certain candle of hope, of promise, of pleasant possibilities, which had flickered with more or less light for so many years, had suddenly gone out and left me alone in utter darkness, as the knowledge was borne in upon me that henceforth Madame de Savaresse had passed altogether and finally out of my life.

And so to-morrow—Brussels!

A CASE OF CONSCIENCE

I

It was in Brittany, and the apples were already acquiring a ruddier, autumnal tint, amid their greens and yellows, though Autumn was not yet; and the country lay very still and fair in the sunset which had befallen, softly and suddenly as is the fashion there. A man and a girl stood looking down in silence at the village, Ploumariel, from their post of vantage, half way up the hill: at its lichened church spire, dotted with little gables, like dove-cotes; at the slated roof of its market; at its quiet white houses. The man's eyes rested on it complacently, with the enjoyment of the painter, finding it charming: the girl's, a little absently, as one who had seen it very often before. She was pretty and very young, but her gray serious eyes, the poise of her head, with its rebellious brown hair braided plainly, gave her a little air of dignity, of reserve which sat piquantly upon her youth. In one ungloved hand, that was brown from the sun, but very beautiful, she held an old parasol, the other played occasionally with a bit of purple heather. Presently she began to speak, using English just coloured by a foreign accent, that made her speech prettier.

'You make me afraid,' she said, turning her large, troubled eyes on her companion, 'you make me afraid, of myself chiefly, but a little of you. You suggest so much to me that is new, strange, terrible. When you speak, I am troubled; all my old landmarks appear to vanish; I even hardly know right from wrong. I love you, my God, how I love you! but I want to go away from you and pray in the little quiet church, where I made my first Communion. I will come to the world's end with you; but oh, Sebastian, do not ask me, let me go. You will forget me, I am a little girl to you, Sebastian. You cannot care very much for me.'

The man looked down at her, smiling masterfully, but very kindly. He took the mutinous hand, with its little sprig of heather, and held it between his own. He seemed to find her insistence adorable; mentally, he was contrasting her with all other women whom he had known, frowning at the memory of so many years in which she had no part. He was a man of more than forty, built large to an uniform English pattern; there was a touch of military erectness in his carriage which often deceived people as to his vocation. Actually, he had never been anything but artist, though he came of a family of soldiers, and had once been war correspondent of an illustrated paper. A certain distinction had always adhered to him, never more than now when he was no longer young, was growing bald, had streaks of gray in his moustache. His face, without being handsome, possessed a certain charm; it was worn and rather pale, the lines about the firm mouth were full of lassitude, the eyes rather tired. He had the air of having tasted widely, curiously, of life in his day, prosperous as he seemed now, that had left its mark upon him. His voice, which usually took an intonation that his friends found supercilious, grew very tender in addressing this little French girl, with her quaint air of childish dignity.

'Marie-Yvonne, foolish child, I will not hear one word more. You are a little heretic; and I am sorely tempted to seal your lips from uttering heresy. You tell me that you love me, and you ask me to let you go, in one breath. The impossible conjuncture! Marie-Yvonne,' he added, more seriously, 'trust yourself to me, my child! You know, I will never give you up. You know that these months that I have been at Ploumariel, are worth all the rest of my life to me. It has been a difficult life, hitherto, little one: change it for me; make it worth while. You would let morbid fancies come between us. You have lived overmuch in that little church, with its worm-eaten benches, and its mildewed odour of dead people, and dead ideas. Take care, Marie-Yvonne: it had made you serious-eyed, before you have learnt to laugh; by and by, it will steal away your youth, before you have ever been young. I come to claim you, Marie-Yvonne, in the name of Life.' His words were half-jesting; his eyes were profoundly in earnest. He drew her to him gently; and when he bent down and kissed her forehead, and then her shy lips, she made no resistance: only, a little tremor ran through her. Presently, with equal gentleness, he put her away from him. 'You have already given me your answer, Marie-Yvonne. Believe me, you will never regret it. Let us go down.'

They took their way in silence towards the village; presently a bend of the road hid them from it, and he drew closer to her, helping her with his arm over the rough stones. Emerging, they had gone thirty yards so, before the scent of English tobacco drew their attention to a figure seated by the road-side, under a hedge; they recognised it, and started apart, a little consciously.

'It is M. Tregellan,' said the young girl, flushing: 'and he must have seen us.'

Her companion, frowning, hardly suppressed a little quick objurgation.

'It makes no matter,' he observed, after a moment: 'I shall see your uncle to-morrow and we know, good man, how he wishes this; and, in any case, I would have told Tregellan.'

The figure rose, as they drew near: he shook the ashes out of his briar, and removed it to his pocket. He was a slight man, with an ugly, clever face; his voice as he greeted them, was very low and pleasant.

'You must have had a charming walk, Mademoiselle. I have seldom seen Ploumariel look better.'

'Yes,' she said, gravely, 'it has been very pleasant. But I must not linger now,' she added breaking a little silence in which none of them seemed quite at ease. 'My uncle will be expecting me to supper.' She held out her hand, in the English fashion, to Tregellan, and then to Sebastian Murch, who gave the little fingers a private pressure.

They had come into the market-place round which most of the houses in Ploumariel were grouped. They watched the young girl cross it briskly; saw her blue gown pass out of sight down a bye street: then they turned to their own hotel. It was a low, white house, belted half way down the front with black stone; a pictorial object, as most Breton hostels. The ground floor was a *café*; and, outside it, a bench and long stained table enticed them to rest. They sat down, and ordered *absinthes*, as the hour suggested: these were brought to them presently by an old servant of the house; an admirable figure, with the white sleeves and apron relieving her linsey dress: with her good Breton face, and its effective wrinkles. For some time they sat in silence, drinking and smoking. The artist appeared to be absorbed in contemplation of his drink; considering its clouded green in various lights. After a while the other looked up, and remarked, abruptly.

'I may as well tell you that I happened to overlook you, just now, unintentionally.'

Sebastian Murch held up his glass, with absent eyes.

'Don't mention it, my dear fellow,' he remarked, at last, urbanely.

'I beg your pardon; but I am afraid I must.'

He spoke with an extreme deliberation which suggested nervousness; with the air of a person reciting a little set speech, learnt imperfectly: and he looked very straight in front of him, out into the street, at two dogs quarrelling over some offal.

'I daresay you will be angry: I can't avoid that; at least, I have known you long enough to hazard it. I have had it on my mind to say something. If I have been silent, it hasn't been because I have been blind, or approved. I have seen how it was all along. I gathered it from your letters when I was in England. Only until this afternoon I did not know how far it had gone, and now I am sorry I did not speak before.'

He stopped short, as though he expected his friend's subtilty to come to his assistance; with admissions or recriminations. But the other was still silent, absent: his face wore a look of annoyed indifference. After a while, as Tregellan still halted, he observed quietly:

'You must be a little more explicit. I confess I miss your meaning.'

'Ah, don't be paltry,' cried the other, quickly. 'You know my meaning. To be very plain, Sebastian, are you quite justified in playing with that charming girl, in compromising her?'

The artist looked up at last, smiling; his expressive mouth was set, not angrily, but with singular determination.

'With Mademoiselle Mitouard?'

'Exactly; with the niece of a man whose guest you have recently been.'

'My dear fellow!' he stopped a little, considering his words: 'You are hasty and uncharitable for such a very moral person! you jump at conclusions, Tregellan. I don't, you know, admit your right to question me: still, as you have introduced the subject, I may as well satisfy you. I have asked Mademoiselle Mitouard to marry me, and she has consented, subject to her uncle's approval. And that her uncle, who happens to prefer the English method of courtship, is not likely to refuse.'

The other held his cigar between two fingers, a little away; his curiously anxious face suggested that the question had become to him one of increased nicety.

'I am sorry,' he said, after a moment; 'this is worse than I imagined; it's impossible.'

'It is you that are impossible, Tregellan,' said Sebastian Murch. He looked at him now, quite frankly, absolutely: his eyes had a defiant light in them, as though he hoped to be criticised; wished nothing better than to stand on his defence, to argue the thing out. And Tregellan sat for a long time without speaking, appreciating his purpose. It seemed more monstrous the closer he considered it: natural enough withal, and so, harder to defeat; and yet, he was sure, that defeated it must be. He reflected how accidental it had all been: their presence there, in Ploumariel, and the rest! Touring in Brittany, as they had often done before, in their habit of old friends, they had fallen upon it by chance, a place unknown of Murray; and the merest chance had held them there. They had slept at the *Lion d'Or*, voted it magnificently picturesque, and would have gone away and forgotten it; but the chance of travel had for once defeated them. Hard by they heard of the little votive chapel of Saint Bernard; at the suggestion of their hostess they set off to visit it. It was built steeply on an edge of rock, amongst odorous pines overhanging a ravine, at the bottom of which they could discern a brown torrent purling tumidly along. For the convenience of devotees, iron rings, at short intervals, were driven into the wall; holding desperately to these, the pious pilgrim, at some peril, might compass the circuit; saying an oraison to Saint Bernard, and some ten *Aves*. Sebastian, who was charmed with the wild beauty of the scene, in a country ordinarily so placid, had been seized with a fit of emulation: not in any mood of devotion, but for the sake of a wider prospect. Tregellan had protested: and the Saint, resenting the purely æsthetic motive of the feat, had seemed to intervene. For, half-way round, growing giddy may be, the artist had made a false step, lost his hold. Tregellan, with a little cry of horror, saw him disappear amidst crumbling mortar and uprooted ferns. It was with a sensible relief, for the fall had the illusion of great depth, that, making his way rapidly down a winding path, he found him lying on a grass terrace, amidst *débris* twenty feet lower, cursing his folly, and holding a lamentably sprained ankle, but for the rest uninjured! Tregellan had made off in haste to Ploumariel in search of assistance; and within the hour he had returned with two stalwart Bretons and M. le Docteur Mitouard.

Their tour had been, naturally, drawing to its close. Tregellan indeed had an imperative need to be in London within the week. It seemed, therefore, a clear dispensation of Providence, that the amiable doctor should prove an hospitable person, and one inspiring confidence no less. Caring greatly for things foreign, and with an especial passion for England, a country whence his brother had brought back a wife; M. le Docteur Mitouard insisted that the invalid could be cared for properly at his house alone. And there, in spite of protestations, earnest from Sebastian, from Tregellan halfhearted, he was installed. And there, two days later, Tregellan left him with an easy mind; bearing away with him, half enviously, the recollection of the young, charming face of a girl, the Doctor's niece, as he had seen her standing by his friend's sofa when he paid his *adieux*; in the beginnings of an intimacy, in which, as he foresaw, the petulance of the invalid, his impatience at an enforced detention, might be considerably forgot. And all that had been two months ago.

II

'I am sorry you don't see it,' continued Tregellan, after a pause, 'to me it seems impossible; considering your history it takes me by surprise.'

The other frowned slightly; finding this persistence perhaps a trifle crude, he remarked good-humouredly enough:

'Will you be good enough to explain your opposition? Do you object to the girl? You have been back a week now, during which you have seen almost as much of her as I.'

'She is a child, to begin with; there is five-and-twenty years' disparity between you. But it's the relation I object to, not the girl. Do you intend to live in Ploumariel?'

Sebastian smiled, with a suggestion of irony.

'Not precisely; I think it would interfere a little with my career; why do you ask?'

'I imagined not; you will go back to London with your little Breton wife, who is as charming here as the apple-blossom in her own garden. You will introduce her to your circle, who will receive her with open arms; all the clever bores, who write, and talk, and paint, and are talked about between Bloomsbury and Kensington. Everybody who is emancipated will know her, and everybody who has a "fad"; and they will come in a body and emancipate her, and teach her their "fads."'

'That is a caricature of my circle, as you call it, Tregellan! though I may remind you it is also yours. I think she is being starved in this corner, spiritually. She has a beautiful soul, and it has had no chance. I propose to give it one, and I am not afraid of the result.'

Tregellan threw away the stump of his cigar into the darkling street, with a little gesture of discouragement, of lassitude.

'She has had the chance to become what she is, a perfect thing.'

'My dear fellow,' exclaimed his friend, 'I could not have said more myself.'

The other continued, ignoring his interruption.

'She has had great luck. She has been brought up by an old eccentric, on the English system of growing up as she liked. And no harm has come of it, at least until it gave you the occasion of making love to her.'

'You are candid, Tregellan!'

'Let her go, Sebastian, let her go,' he continued, with increasing gravity. 'Consider what a transplantation; from this world of Ploumariel where everything is fixed for her by that venerable old *Curé*, where life is so easy, so ordered, to yours, ours; a world without definitions, where everything is an open question.'

'Exactly,' said the artist, 'why should she be so limited? I would give her scope, ideas. I can't see that I am wrong.'

'She will not accept them, your ideas. They will trouble her, terrify her; in the end, divide you. It is not an elastic nature. I have watched it.'

'At least, allow me to know her,' put in the artist, a little grimly.

Tregellan shook his head.

'The Breton blood; her English mother: passionate Catholicism! a touch of Puritan! Have you quite made up your mind, Sebastian?'

'I made it up long ago, Tregellan!'

The other looked at him, curiously, compassionately; with a touch of resentment at what he found his lack of subtilty. Then he said at last:

'I called it impossible; you force me to be very explicit, even cruel. I must remind you, that you are, of all my friends, the one I value most, could least afford to lose.'

'You must be going to say something extremely disagreeable! something horrible,' said the artist, slowly.

'I am,' said Tregellan, 'but I must say it. Have you explained to Mademoiselle, or her uncle, your—your peculiar position?'

Sebastian was silent for a moment, frowning: the lines about his mouth grew a little sterner; at last he said coldly:

'If I were to answer, Yes?'

'Then I should understand that there was no further question of your marriage.'

74

Presently the other commenced in a hard, leaden voice.

'No, I have not told Marie-Yvonne that. I shall not tell her. I have suffered enough for a youthful folly; an act of mad generosity. I refuse to allow an infamous woman to wreck my future life as she has disgraced my past. Legally, she has passed out of it; morally, legally, she is not my wife. For all I know she may be actually dead.'

The other was watching his face, very gray and old now, with an anxious compassion.

'You know she is not dead, Sebastian,' he said simply. Then he added very quietly as one breaks supreme bad tidings, 'I must tell you something which I fear you have not realised. The Catholic Church does not recognise divorce. If she marry you and find out, rightly or wrongly, she will believe that she has been living in sin; some day she will find it out. No damnable secret like that keeps itself for ever: an old newspaper, a chance remark from one of your dear friends, and the deluge. Do you see the tragedy, the misery of it? By God, Sebastian, to save you both somebody shall tell her; and if it be not you, it must be I.'

There was extremest peace in the quiet square; the houses seemed sleepy at last, after a day of exhausting tranquillity, and the chestnuts, under which a few children, with tangled hair and fair dirty faces, still played. The last glow of the sun fell on the gray roofs opposite; dying hard it seemed over the street in which the Mitouards lived; and they heard suddenly the tinkle of an *Angelus* bell. Very placid! the place and the few peasants in their pictorial hats and caps who lingered. Only the two Englishmen sitting, their glasses empty, and their smoking over, looking out on it all with their anxious faces, brought in a contrasting note of modern life; of the complex aching life of cities, with its troubles and its difficulties.

'Is that your final word, Tregellan?' asked the artist at last, a little wearily.

'It must be, Sebastian! Believe me, I am infinitely sorry.'

'Yes, of course,' he answered quickly, acidly; 'well, I will sleep on it.'

III

They made their first breakfast in an almost total silence; both wore the bruised harassed air which tells of a night passed without benefit of sleep. Immediately afterwards Murch went out alone: Tregellan could guess the direction of his visit, but not its object; he wondered if the artist was making his difficult confession. Presently they brought him in a pencilled note; he recognised, with some surprise, his friend's tortuous hand.

'I have considered our conversation, and your unjustifiable interference. I am entirely in your hands: at the mercy of your extraordinary notions of duty. Tell her what you will, if you must; and pave the way to your own success. I shall say nothing; but I swear you love the girl yourself; and are no right arbiter here. Sebastian Murch.'

He read the note through twice before he grasped its purport; then sat holding it in lax fingers, his face grown singularly gray.

'It's not true, it's not true,' he cried aloud, but a moment later knew himself for a self-deceiver all along. Never had self-consciousness been more sudden, unexpected, or complete. There was no more to do or say; this knowledge tied his hands. *Ite! missa est!...*

He spent an hour painfully invoking casuistry, tossed to and fro irresolutely, but never for a moment disputing that plain fact which Sebastian had so brutally illuminated. Yes! he loved her, had loved her all along. Marie-Yvonne! how the name expressed her! at once sweet and serious, arch and sad as her nature. The little Breton wild flower! how cruel it seemed to gather her! And he could do no more; Sebastian had tied his hands. Things must be! He was a man nicely conscientious, and now all the elaborate devices of his honour, which had persuaded him to a disagreeable interference, were contraposed against him. This suspicion of an ulterior motive had altered it, and so at last he was left to decide with a sigh, that because he loved these two so well, he must let them go their own way to misery.

Coming in later in the day, Sebastian Murch found his friend packing.

'I have come to get your answer,' he said; 'I have been walking about the hills like a madman for hours. I have not been near her; I am afraid. Tell me what you mean to do?'

Tregellan rose, shrugged his shoulders, pointed to his valise.

'God help you both! I would have saved you if you had let me. The Quimperlé *Courrier* passes in half-an-hour. I am going by it. I shall catch a night train to Paris.'

As Sebastian said nothing; continued to regard him with the same dull, anxious gaze, he went on after a moment:

'You did me a grave injustice; you should have known me better than that. God knows I meant nothing shameful, only the best; the least misery for you and her.'

'It was true then?' said Sebastian, curiously. His voice was very cold; Tregellan found him altered. He regarded the thing as it had been very remote, and outside them both.

'I did not know it then,' said Tregellan, shortly.

He knelt down again and resumed his packing. Sebastian, leaning against the bed, watched him with absent intensity, which was yet alive to trivial things, and he handed him from time to time a book, a brush, which the other packed mechanically with elaborate care. There was no more to say, and presently, when the chambermaid entered for his luggage, they went down and out into the splendid sunshine, silently. They had to cross the Square to reach the carriage, a dusty ancient vehicle, hooded, with places for four, which waited outside the postoffice. A man in a blue blouse preceded them, carrying Tregellan's things. From the corner they could look down the road to Quimperlé, and their eyes both sought the white house of Doctor Mitouard, standing back a little in its trim garden, with its one incongruous apple tree; but there was no one visible.

Presently, Sebastian asked, suddenly:

'Is it true, that you said last night: divorce to a Catholic—?'

Tregellan interrupted him.

'It is absolutely true, my poor friend.'

He had climbed into his place at the back, settled himself on the shiny leather cushion: he appeared to be the only passenger. Sebastian stood looking drearily in at the window, the glass of which had long perished.

'I wish I had never known, Tregellan! How could I ever tell her!'

Inside, Tregellan shrugged his shoulders: not impatiently, or angrily, but in sheer impotence; as one who gave it up.

'I can't help you,' he said, 'you must arrange it with your own conscience.'

'Ah, it's too difficult!' cried the other: 'I can't find my way.'

The driver cracked his whip, suggestively; Sebastian drew back a little further from the off wheel.

'Well,' said the other, 'if you find it, write and tell me. I am very sorry, Sebastian.'

'Good-bye,' he replied. 'Yes! I will write.'

The carriage lumbered off, with a lurch to the right, as it turned the corner; it rattled down the hill, raising a cloud of white dust. As it passed the Mitouards' house, a young girl, in a large straw hat, came down the garden, too late to discover whom it contained. She watched it out of sight, indifferently, leaning on the little iron gate; then she turned, to recognize the long stooping figure of Sebastian Murch, who advanced to meet her.

AN ORCHESTRAL VIOLIN

I

At my dining-place in old Soho—I call it mine because there was a time when I became somewhat inveterate there, keeping my napkin (changed once a week) in a ring recognisable by myself and the waiter, my bottle of Beaune (replenished more frequently), and my accustomed seat—at this restaurant of mine, with its confusion of tongues, its various, foreign *clientèle*, amid all the coming and going, the nightly change of faces, there were some which remained the same, persons with whom, though one might never have spoken, one had nevertheless from the mere continuity of juxtaposition a certain sense of intimacy.

There was one old gentleman in particular, as inveterate as myself, who especially aroused my interest. A courteous, punctual, mild old man with an air which deprecated notice; who conversed each evening for a minute or two with the proprietor, as he rolled, always at the same hour, a valedictory cigarette, in a language that arrested my ear by its strangeness; and which proved to be his own, Hungarian; who addressed a brief remark to me at times, half apologetically, in the precisest of English. We sat next each other at the same table, came and went at much the same hour; and for a long while our intercourse was restricted to formal courtesies; mutual inquiries after each other's health, a few urbane strictures on the climate. The little old gentleman in spite of his aspect of shabby gentility,—for his coat was sadly inefficient, and the nap of his carefully brushed hat did not indicate prosperity—perhaps even because of this suggestion of fallen fortunes, bore himself with pathetic erectness, almost haughtily. He did not seem amenable to advances. It was a long time before I knew him well enough to value rightly this appearance, the timid defences, behind which a very shy and delicate nature took refuge from the world's coarse curiosity. I can smile now, with a certain sadness, when I remind myself that at one time I was somewhat in awe of M. Maurice Cristich and his little air of proud humility. Now that his place in that dim, foreign eating-house knows him no more, and his yellow napkin-ring, with its distinguishing number, has been passed on to some other customer; I have it in my mind to set down my impressions of him, the short history of our acquaintance. It began with an exchange of cards; a form to which he evidently attached a ceremonial value, for after that piece of ritual his manner underwent a sensible softening, and he showed by many subtle indefinable shades in his courteous address, that he did me the honour of including me in his friendship. I have his card before me now; a large, oblong piece of pasteboard, with *M. Maurice Cristich, Theatre Royal*, inscribed upon it, amid many florid flourishes. It enabled me to form my first definite notion of his calling, upon which I had previously wasted much conjecture; though I had all along, and rightly as it appeared, associated him in some manner with music.

In time he was good enough to inform me further. He was a musician, a violinist; and formerly, and in his own country, he had been a composer. But whether for some lack in him of original talent, or of patience, whether for some grossness in the public taste, on which the nervous delicacy and refinement of his execution was lost, he had not continued. He had been driven by poverty to London, had given lessons, and then for many years had played a second violin in the orchestra of the Opera.

'It is not much, Monsieur!' he observed, deprecatingly, smoothing his hat with the cuff of his frayed coat-sleeve. 'But it is sufficient; and I prefer it to teaching. In effect, they are very charming, the seraphic young girls of your country! But they seem to care little for music; and I am a difficult master, and have not enough patience. Once, you see, a long time ago, I had a perfect pupil, and perhaps that spoilt me. Yes! I prefer the theatre, though it is less profitable. It is not as it once was,' he added, with a half sigh; 'I am no longer ambitious. Yes, Monsieur, when I was young, I was ambitious. I wrote a symphony and several concertos. I even brought out at Vienna an opera, which I thought would make me famous; but the good folk of Vienna did not appreciate me, and they would have none of my music. They said it was antiquated, my opera, and absurd; and yet, it seemed to me good. I think that Gluck, that great genius, would have liked it; and that is what I should have wished. Ah! how long ago it seems, that time when I was ambitious! But you must excuse me, Monsieur! your good company makes me garrulous. I must be at the theatre. If I am not in my place at the half-hour, they fine me two shillings and sixpence, and that I can ill afford, you know, Monsieur!'

In spite of his defeats, his long and ineffectual struggle with adversity, M. Cristich, I discovered, as our acquaintance ripened, had none of the spleen and little of the vanity of the unsuccessful artist. He seemed in his forlorn old age to have accepted his discomfiture with touching resignation, having acquired neither cynicism nor indifference. He was simply an innocent old man, in love with his violin and with his art, who had acquiesced in disappointment; and it was impossible to decide, whether he even believed in his talent, or had not silently accredited the verdict of musical Vienna, which had condemned his opera in those days when he was ambitious. The precariousness of the London Opera was the one fact which I ever knew to excite him to expressions of personal resentment. When its doors were closed, his hard poverty (it was the only occasion when he protested against it), drove him, with his dear instrument and his accomplished fingers, into the orchestras of lighter houses, where he was compelled to play music which he despised. He grew silent and rueful during these periods of irksome servitude, rolled innumerable cigarettes, which he smoked with fierceness and great rapidity. When dinner was done, he was often volubly indignant, in Hungarian, to the proprietor. But with the beginning of the season his mood lightened. He bore himself more sprucely, and would leave me, to assist at a representation of *Don Giovanni*, or *Tannhauser*, with a face which was almost radiant. I had known him a year before it struck me that I should like to see him in his professional capacity. I told him of my desire a little diffidently, not knowing how my purpose might strike him. He responded graciously, but with an air of intrigue, laying a gentle hand upon my coat sleeve and bidding me wait. A day or two later, as we sat over our coffee, M. Cristich with an hesitating urbanity offered me an order.

'If you would do me the honour to accept it, Monsieur! It is a stall, and a good one! I have never asked for one before, all these years, so they gave it to me easily. You see, I have few friends. It is for to-morrow, as you observe, I demanded it especially; it is an occasion of great interest to me,—ah! an occasion! You will come?'

'You are too good, M. Cristich!' I said with genuine gratitude, for indeed the gift came in season, the opera being at that time a luxury I could seldom command. 'Need I say that I shall be delighted? And to hear Madame Romanoff, a chance one has so seldom!'

The old gentleman's mild, dull eyes glistened. 'Madame Romanoff!' he repeated, 'the marvellous Leonora! yes, yes! She has sung only once before in London. Ah, when I remember—' He broke off suddenly. As he rose, and prepared for departure, he held my hand a little longer than usual, giving it a more intimate pressure.

'My dear young friend, will you think me a presumptuous old man, if I ask you to come and see me to-morrow in my apartment, when it is over? I will give you a glass of whisky, and we will smoke pipes, and you shall tell me your impressions—and then I will tell you why to-morrow I shall be so proud, why I show this emotion.'

II

The Opera was *Fidelio*, that stately, splendid work, whose melody, if one may make a pictorial comparison, has something of that rich and sun-warm colour which, certainly, on the canvasses of Rubens, affects one as an almost musical quality. It offered brilliant opportunities, and the incomparable singer had wasted none of them. So that when, at last, I pushed my way out of the crowded house and joined M. Cristich at the stage door, where he waited with eyes full of expectancy, the music still lingered about me, like the faint, past fragrance of incense, and I had no need to speak my thanks. He rested a light hand on my arm, and we walked towards his lodging silently; the musician carrying his instrument in its sombre case, and shivering from time to time, a tribute to the keen spring night. He stooped as he walked, his eyes trailing the ground; and a certain listlessness in his manner struck me a little strangely, as though he came fresh from some solemn or hieratic experience, of which the reaction had already begun to set in tediously, leaving him at the last unstrung and jaded, a little weary, of himself and the too strenuous occasion. It was not until we had crossed the threshold of a dingy, high house in a byway of Bloomsbury, and he had ushered me, with apologies, into his shabby room, near the sky, that the sense of his hospitable duties seemed to renovate him. He produced tumblers from an obscure recess behind his bed; set a kettle on the fire, a lodging-house fire, which scarcely smouldered with flickers of depressing, sulphurous flame, talking of indifferent subjects, as he watched for it to boil.

Only when we had settled ourselves, in uneasy chairs, opposite each other, and he had composed me, what he termed 'a grog': himself preferring the more innocent mixture known as *eau sucrée*, did he allude to *Fidelio*. I praised heartily the discipline of the orchestra, the prima donna, whom report made his country-woman, with her strong, sweet voice and her extraordinary beauty, the magnificence of the music, the fine impression of the whole.

M. Cristich, his glass in hand, nodded approval. He looked intently into the fire, which cast mocking shadows over his quaint, incongruous figure, his antiquated dress coat, which seemed to skimp him, his frost-bitten countenance, his cropped grey hair. 'Yes,' he said, 'Yes! So it pleased you, and you thought her beautiful? I am glad.'

He turned round to me abruptly, and laid a thin hand impressively on my knee.

'You know I invented her, the Romanoff, discovered her, taught her all she learnt. Yes, Monsieur, I was proud to-night, very proud, to be there, playing for her, though she did not know. Ah! the beautiful creature!… and how badly I played! execrably! You could not notice that, Monsieur, but they did, my confrères, and could not understand. How should they? How should they dream, that I, Maurice Cristich, second violin in the orchestra of the opera, had to do with the Leonora; even I! Her voice thrilled them; ah, but it was I who taught her her notes! They praised her diamonds; yes, but once I gave her that she wanted more than diamonds, bread, and lodging and love. Beautiful they called her; she was beautiful too, when I carried her in my arms through Vienna. I am an old man now, and good for very little; and there have been days, God forgive me! when I have been angry with her; but it was not to-night. To see her there, so beautiful and so great; and to feel that after all I had a hand in it, that I invented her. Yes, yes! I had my

79

victory to-night too; though it was so private; a secret between you and me, Monsieur? Is it not?'

I assured him of my discretion, but he hardly seemed to hear. His sad eyes had wandered away to the live coals, and he considered them pensively, as though he found them full of charming memories. I sat back, respecting his remoteness; but my silence was replete with surprised conjecture, and indeed the quaint figure of the old musician, every line of his garments redolent of ill success, had become to me, of a sudden, strangely romantic. Destiny, so amorous of surprises, of pathetic or cynical contrasts, had in this instance excelled herself. My obscure acquaintance, Maurice Cristich! The renowned Romanoff! Her name and acknowledged genius had been often in men's mouths of late, a certain luminous, scarcely sacred, glamour attaching to it, in an hundred idle stories, due perhaps as much to the wonder of her sorrowful beauty, as to any justification in knowledge, of her boundless extravagance, her magnificent fantasies, her various perversity, rumour pointing specially at those priceless diamonds, the favours not altogether gratuitous it was said of exalted personages. And with all deductions made, for malice, for the ingenuity of the curious, the impression of her perversity was left; she remained enigmatical and notorious, a somewhat scandalous heroine! And Cristich had known her; he had, as he declared, and his accent was not that of bragadoccio, invented her. The conjuncture puzzled and fascinated me. It did not make Cristich less interesting, nor the prima-donna more perspicuous.

By-and-by the violinist looked up at me; he smiled with a little dazed air, as though his thoughts had been a far journey.

'Pardon me, Monsieur! I beg you to fill your glass. I seem a poor host; but to tell you the truth, I was dreaming; I was quite away, quite away.'

He threw out his hands, with a vague expansive gesture.

'Dear child!' he said to the flames, in French; 'good little one! I do not forget thee.' And he began to tell me.

'It was when I was at Vienna, ah! a long while ago. I was not rich, but neither was I very poor; I still had my little patrimony, and I lived in the —— Strasse, very economically; it is a quarter which many artists frequent. I husbanded my resources, that I might be able to work away at my art without the tedium of making it a means of livelihood. I refused many offers to play in public, that I might have more leisure. I should not do that now; but then, I was very confident; I had great faith in me. And I worked very hard at my symphony, and I was full of desire to write an opera. It was a tall dark house, where I lived; there were many other lodgers, but I knew scarcely any of them. I went about with my head full of music and I had my violin; I had no time to seek acquaintance. Only my neighbour, at the other side of my passage, I knew slightly and bowed to him when we met on the stairs. He was a dark, lean man, of a very distinguished air; he must have lived very hard, he had death in his face. He was not an artist, like the rest of us; I suspect he was a great profligate, and a gambler; but he had the manners of a gentleman. And when I came to talk to him, he displayed the greatest knowledge of music that I have ever known. And it was the same with all; he talked divinely, of everything in the world, but very wildly and bitterly. He seemed to have been everywhere, and done everything; and at last to be tired of it all; and of himself the most. From the people of the house I heard that he was a Pole; noble, and very poor; and, what surprised me, that he had a daughter with him, a little girl. I used to pity this child, who must have lived quite alone. For the Count was always out, and the child never appeared with him; and, for the rest, with his black spleen and tempers, he must have been but sorry company for a little girl. I wished much to see her, for you see, Monsieur! I am fond of children, almost as much as of music; and one day it came about. I was at home with my violin; I had been playing all the evening some songs I had made; and once or twice I had seemed to be interrupted by little, tedious sounds. At last I stopped, and opened the door; and there, crouching down, I found the most beautiful little creature I had ever seen in my life. It was the child of my neighbour. Yes, Monsieur! you divine, you divine! That was the Leonora!'

'And she is not your compatriot,' I asked.

'A Hungarian? ah, no! yet every piece of her pure Slav. But I weary you, Monsieur; I make a long story.'

I protested my interest; and after a little side glance of dubious scrutiny, he continued in a constrained monotone, as one who told over to himself some rosary of sad enchanting memories.

'Ah, yes! she was beautiful; that mysterious, sad Slavonic beauty! a thing quite special and apart. And, as a child, it was more tragical and strange; that dusky hair! those profound and luminous eyes! seeming to mourn over tragedies they have never known. A strange, wild, silent child! She might have been eight or nine, then; but her little soul was hungry for music. It was a veritable passion; and when she became at last my good friend, she told me how often she had lain for long hours outside my door, listening to my violin. I gave her a kind of scolding, such as one could to so beautiful a little creature, for the passage was draughty and cold, and sent her away with some *bon-bons*. She shook back her long, dark hair: 'You are not angry, and I am not naughty,' she said: 'and I shall come back. I thank you for your *bon-bons*; but I like your music better than *bon-bons*, or fairy tales, or anything in the world.'

'But she never came back to the passage again, Monsieur! The next time I came across the Count, I sent her an invitation, a little diffidently, for he had never spoken to me of her, and he was a strange and difficult man. Now, he simply shrugged his shoulders, with a smile, in which, for once, there seemed more entertainment than malice. The child could visit me when she chose; if it amused either of us, so much the better. And we were content, and she came to me often; after a while, indeed, she was with me almost always. Child as she was, she had already the promise of her magnificent voice; and I taught her to use it, to sing, and to play on the piano and on the violin, to which she took the most readily. She was like a singing bird in the room, such pure, clear notes! And she grew very fond of me; she would fall asleep at last in my arms, and so stay until the Count would take her with him when he entered, long after midnight. He came to me naturally for her soon; and they never seemed long those hours that I watched over her sleep. I never knew him harsh or unkind to the child; he seemed simply indifferent to her as to everything else. He had exhausted life and he hated it; and he knew that death was on him, and he hated that even more. And yet he was careful of her after a fashion, buying her *bon-bons* and little costumes, when he was in the vein, pitching his voice softly when he would stay and talk to me, as though he relished her sleep. One night he did not come to fetch her at all, I had wrapped a blanket round the child where she lay on my bed, and had sat down to watch by her and presently I too fell asleep. I do not know how long I slept but when I woke there was a gray light in the room, I was very cold and stiff, but I could hear close by, the soft, regular breathing of the child. There was a great uneasiness on me, and after a while I stole out across the passage and knocked at the Count's door, there was no answer but it gave when I tried it, and so I went in. The lamp had smouldered out, there was a sick odour of *pétrol* everywhere, and the shutters were closed: but through the chinks the merciless gray dawn streamed in and showed me the Count sitting very still by the table. His face wore a most curious smile, and had not his great cavernous eyes been open, I should have believed him asleep: suddenly it came to me that he was dead. He was not a good man, monsieur, nor an amiable, but a true *virtuoso* and full of information, and I grieved. I have had Masses said for the repose of his soul.'

81

He paid a tribute of silence to the dead man's memory, and then he went on.

'It seemed quite natural that I should take his child. There was no one to care, no one to object; it happened quite easily. We went, the little one and I, to another part of the city. We made quite a new life. Oh! my God! it is a very long time ago.'

Quite suddenly his voice went tremulous; but after a pause, hardly perceptible, he recovered himself and continued with an accent of apology.

'I am a foolish old man, and very garrulous. It is not good to think of that, nor to talk of it; I do not know why I do. But what would you have? She loved me then, and she had the voice and the disposition of an angel. I have never been very happy. I think sometimes, monsieur, that we others, who care much for art, are not permitted that. But certainly those few, rapid days, when she was a child, were good; and yet they were the days of my defeat. I found myself out then. I was never to be a great artist, a *maestro*: a second-rate man, a good music-teacher for young ladies, a capable performer in an orchestra, what you will, but a great artist, never! Yet in those days, even when my opera failed, I had consolation, I could say, I have a child! I would have kept her with me always but it could not be, from the very first she would be a singer. I knew always that a day would come when she would not need me, she was meant to be the world's delight, and I had no right to keep her, even if I could. I held my beautiful, strange bird in her cage, until she beat her wings against the bars, then I opened the door. At the last, I think, that is all we can do for our children, our best beloved, our very heart-strings, stand free of them, let them go. The world is very weary, but we must all find that out for ourselves, perhaps when they are tired they will come home, perhaps not, perhaps not. It was to the Conservatoire, at Milan, that I sent her finally, and it was at La Scala that she afterwards appeared, and at La Scala too, poor child, she met her evil genius, the man named Romanoff, a baritone in her company, own son of the devil, whom she married. Ah, if I could have prevented it, if I could have prevented it!'

He lapsed into a long silence; a great weariness seemed to have come over him, and in the gray light which filtered in through the dingy window blinds, his face was pinched and wasted, unutterably old and forlorn.

'But I did not prevent it,' he said at last, 'for all my good will, perhaps merely hastened it by unseasonable interference. And so we went in different ways, with anger I fear, and at least with sore hearts and misunderstanding.'

He spoke with an accent of finality, and so sadly that in a sudden rush of pity I was moved to protest.

'But, surely you meet sometimes; surely this woman, who was as your own child—'

He stopped me with a solemn, appealing gesture.

'You are young, and you do not altogether understand. You must not judge her; you must not believe, that she forgets, that she does not care. Only, it is better like this, because it could never be as before. I could not help her. I want nothing that she can give me, no not anything; I have my memories! I hear of her, from time to time; I hear what the world says of her, the imbecile world, and I smile. Do I not know best? I, who carried her in my arms, when she was that high!'

And in effect the old violinist smiled, it was as though he had surprised my secret of dissatisfaction, and found it, like the malice of the world, too ignorant to resent. The edge of his old, passionate adoration had remained bright and keen through the years; and it imparted a strange brilliancy to his eyes, which half convinced me, as presently, with a resumption of his usual air of diffident courtesy, he ushered me out into the vague, spring dawn. And yet, when I had parted from him and was making my way somewhat wearily to my own quarters, my first dubious impression remained. My imagination was busy with the story I had heard, striving quite vainly to supply omissions, to fill in meagre outlines. Yes! quite vainly! the figure of the Romanoff was left, ambiguous and unexplained; hardly acquitted in my mind of a certain callousness, an ingratitude almost vulgar as it started out from time to time, in contraposition against that forlorn old age.

III

I saw him once more at the little restaurant in Soho, before a sudden change of fortune, calling me abroad for an absence, as it happened, of years, closed the habit of our society. He gave me the god-speed of a brother artist, though mine was not the way of music, with many prophesies of my success; and the pressure of his hand, as he took leave of me, was tremulous.

'I am an old man, monsieur, and we may not meet again, in this world. I wish you all the chances you deserve in Paris; but I—I shall greatly miss you. If you come back in time, you will find me in the old places; and if not—there are things of mine, which I should wish you to have, that shall be sent you.'

And indeed it proved to be our last meeting. I went to Paris; a fitful correspondence intervened, grew infrequent, ceased; then a little later, came to me the notification, very brief and official, of his death in the French Hospital of pneumonia. It was followed by a few remembrances of him, sent at his request, I learnt, by the priest who had administered to him the last offices: some books that he had greatly cherished, works of Glück, for the most part; an antique ivory crucifix of very curious workmanship; and his violin, a beautiful instrument dated 1670 and made at Nuremberg, yet with a tone which seemed to me, at least, as fine as that of the Cremonas. It had an intrinsic value to me, apart from its associations; for I too was something of an amateur, and since this seasoned melodious wood had come into my possession, I was inspired to take my facility more seriously. To play in public, indeed, I had neither leisure nor desire: but in certain *salons* of my acquaintance, where music was much in vogue, I made from time to time a desultory appearance. I set down these facts, because as it happened, this ineffectual talent of mine, which poor Cristich's legacy had recalled to life, was to procure me an interesting encounter. I remember the occasion well, it was too appropriate to be forgotten—as though my old friend's lifeless fiddle, which had yet survived so many *maestri*, was to be a direct instrument of the completion of his story, the resurrection of those dormant and unsatisfied curiosities which still now and again concerned me. I had played at an house where I was a stranger; brought there by a friend, to whose insistence I had yielded somewhat reluctantly; although he had assured me, and, I believe, with reason, that it was a house where the indirect, or Attic invitation greatly prevailed, in brief, a place where one met very queer people. The hostess was American, a charming woman, of unimpeachable antecedents; but her passion for society, which, while it should always be interesting, was not always equally reputable, had exposed her evenings to the suspicion of her compatriots. And when I had discharged my part in the programme and had leisure to look around me, I saw at a glance that their suspicion was justified; very queer people indeed were there. The large hot rooms were cosmopolitan: infidels and Jews, everybody and nobody; a scandalously promiscuous assemblage! And there, with a half start, which was not at first recognition, my eyes stopped before a face which brought to me a confused rush of memories. It was that of a woman who sat on an ottoman in the smallest room which was almost empty. Her companion was a small, vivacious man with a gray imperial, and the red ribbon in his buttonhole, to whose continuous stream of talk, eked out with meridional gestures, she had the air of being listlessly resigned. Her dress, a marvel of discretion, its colour the yellow of old ivory, was of some very rich and stiff stuff cut square to her neck; that, and her great black hair, clustered to a crimson rose at the top of her head, made the pallor of her face a thing to

83

marvel at. Her beauty was at once sombre and illuminating, and youthful no less. The woman of thirty: but her complexion, and her arms, which were bare, were soft in texture as a young girl's.

I made my way as well as I could for the crowd, to my hostess, listened, with what patience I might, to some polite praise of my playing, and made my request.

'Mrs. Destrier, I have an immense favour to ask; introduce me to Madame Romanoff!'

She gave me a quick, shrewd smile; then I remembered stories of her intimate quaintness.

'My dear young man! I have no objection. Only I warn you, she is not conversational; you will make no good of it, and you will be disappointed; perhaps that will be best. Please remember, I am responsible for nobody.'

'Is she so dangerous?' I asked. 'But never mind; I believe that I have something to say which may interest her.'

'Oh, for that!' she smiled elliptically; 'yes, she is most dangerous. But I will introduce you; you shall tell me how you succeed.'

I bowed and smiled; she laid a light hand on my arm; and I piloted her to the desired corner. It seemed that the chance was with me. The little fluent Provençal had just vacated his seat; and when the prima-donna had acknowledged the hasty mention of my name, with a bare inclination of her head, I was emboldened to succeed to it. And then I was silent. In the perfection of that dolorous face, I could not but be reminded of the tradition which has always ascribed something fatal and inevitable to the possession of great gifts: of genius or uncommon fortune, or singular personal beauty; and the common-place of conversation failed me.

After a while she looked askance at me, with a sudden flash of resentment.

'You speak no French, Monsieur! And yet you write it well enough; I have read your stories.'

I acknowledged Madame's irony, permitted myself to hope that my efforts had met with Madame's approval.

'*A la bonne heure!* I perceive you also speak it. Is that why you wished to be presented, to hear my criticisms?'

'Let me answer that question when you have answered mine.'

She glanced curiously over her feathered fan, then with the slightest upward inclination of her statuesque shoulders—'I admire your books; but are your women quite just? I prefer your playing.'

'That is better, Madame! It was to talk of that I came.'

'Your playing?'

'My violin.'

'You want me to look at it? It is a Cremona?'

'It is not a Cremona; but if you like, I will give it you.'

Her dark eyes shone out in amazed amusement.

'You are eccentric, Monsieur! but your nation has a privilege of eccentricity. At least, you amuse me; and I have wearied myself enough this long evening. Show me your violin; I am something of a *virtuosa*.'

I took the instrument from its case, handed it to her in silence, watching her gravely. She received it with the dexterous hands of a musician, looked at the splendid stains on the back, then bent over towards the light in a curious scrutiny of the little, faded signature of its maker, the *fecit* of an obscure Bavarian of the seventeenth century; and it was a long time before she raised her eyes.

When she spoke, her rich voice had a note of imperious entreaty in it. 'Your violin interests me, Monsieur! Oh, I know that wood! It came to you—?'

'A legacy from an esteemed friend.'

She shot back. 'His name?' with the flash which I waited for.

'Maurice Cristich, Madame!'

We were deserted in our corner. The company had strayed in, one by one, to the large *salon* with the great piano, where a young Russian musician, a pupil of Chopin, sat down to play, with no conventional essay of preliminary chords, an expected morsel. The strains of it wailed in just then, through the heavy, screening curtains; a mad *valse* of his own, that no human feet could dance to, a pitiful, passionate thing that thrilled the nerves painfully, ringing the changes between voluptuous sorrow and the merriment of devils, and burdened always with the weariness of 'all the Russias,' the proper *Welt-schmerz* of a young, disconsolate people. It seemed to charge the air, like electricity, with passionate undertones; it gave intimate facilities, and a tense personal note to our interview.

'A legacy! so he is gone.' She swayed to me with a wail in her voice, in a sort of childish abandonment: 'and *you* tell me! Ah!' she drew back, chilling suddenly with a touch of visible suspicion. 'You hurt me, Monsieur! Is it a stroke at random? You spoke of a gift; you say you knew, esteemed him. You were with him? Perhaps, a message …?'

'He died alone, Madame! I have no message. If there were none, it might be, perhaps, that he believed you had not cared for it. If that were wrong, I could tell you that you were not forgotten. Oh! he loved you! I had his word for it, and the story. The violin is yours—do not mistake me; it is not for your sake but his. He died alone; value it, as I should, Madame!'

They were insolent words, perhaps cruel, provoked from me by the mixed nature of my attraction to her; the need of turning a reasonable and cool front to that pathetic beauty, that artful music, which whipped jaded nerves to mutiny. The arrow in them struck so true, that I was shocked at my work. It transfixed the child in her, latent in most women, which moaned at my feet; so that for sheer shame as though it were actually a child I had hurt, I could have fallen and kissed her hands.

'Oh, you judge me hard, you believe the worst of me and why not? I am against the world! At least he might have taught you to be generous, that kind old man! Have I forgotten do you think! Am I so happy then? Oh it is a just question, the world busies itself with me, and you are in the lap of its tongues. Has it ever accused me of that, of happiness? Cruel, cruel! I have paid my penalties, and a woman is not free to do as she will, but would not I have gone to him, for a word, a sign? Yes, for the sake of my childhood. And to-night when you showed me that,' her white hand swept over the violin with something of a caress, 'I thought it had come, yes, from the grave, and you make it more bitter by readings of your own. You strike me hard.'

I bent forward in real humility, her voice had tears in it, though her splendid eyes were hard.

'Forgive me, Madame! a vulgar stroke at random. I had no right to make it, he told me only good of you. Forgive me, and for proof of your pardon—I am serious now—take his violin.'

Her smile, as she refused me, was full of sad dignity.

'You have made it impossible, Monsieur! It would remind me only now of how ill you think of me. I beg you to keep it.'

The music had died away suddenly, and its ceasing had been followed by a loud murmur of applause. The prima-donna rose, and stood for a moment observing me, irresolutely.

'I leave you and your violin, Monsieur! I have to sing presently, with such voice as our talk has left me. I bid you both adieu!'

'Ah, Madame!' I deprecated, 'you will think again of this, I will send it you in the morning. I have no right....'

She shook her head, then with a sudden flash of amusement, or fantasy—'I agree, Monsieur! on a condition. To prove your penitence, you shall bring it to me yourself.'

I professed that her favour overpowered me. She named an hour when she would be at home: an address in the Avenue des Champs Elysées, which I noted on my tablets.

'Not adieu then, Monsieur! but *au revoir.*'

I bowed perplexedly, holding the curtain aside to let her sweep through; and once more she turned back, gathering up her voluminous train, to repeat with a glance and accent, which I found mystifying: 'Remember, Monsieur! It is only *au revoir.*'

That last glimpse of her, with the strange mockery and an almost elfish malice in her fine eyes, went home with me later to cause vague disquiet and fresh suspicion of her truth. The spell of her extraordinary, personal charm removed, doubt would assert itself. Was she quite sincere? Was her fascination not a questionable one? Might not that almost childish outburst of a grief so touching, and at the time convincing, be after all factitious; the movement of a born actress and enchantress of men, quick to seize as by a nice professional instinct the opportunity of an effect? Had her whole attitude been a deliberate pose, a sort of trick? The sudden changes in her subtile voice, the under current of mockery in an invitation which seemed inconsequent, put me on my guard, reinforced all my deep-seated prejudices against the candor of the feminine soul. It left me with a vision of her, fantastically vivid, raccounting to an intimate circle, to an accompaniment of some discreet laughter and the popping of champagne corks, the success of her imposition, the sentimental concessions which she had extorted from a notorious student of cynical moods.

A dangerous woman! cried Mrs. Destrier with the world, which might conceivably be right; at least I was fain to add, a woman whose laughter would be merciless. Certainly, I had no temper for adventures; and a visit to Madame Romanoff on so sentimental an errand seemed to me, the more I pondered it, to partake of this quality to be rich in distasteful possibilities. Must I write myself pusillanimous, if I confess that I never made it, that I committed my old friend's violin into the hands of the woman who had been his pupil by the vulgar aid of a *commissionaire*?

Pusillanimous or simply prudent; or perhaps cruelly unjust, to a person who had paid penalties and greatly needed kindness? It is a point I have never been able to decide, though I have tried to raise theories on the ground of her acquiescence. It seemed to me on the cards, that my fiddle bestowed so cavalierly, should be refused. And yet even the fact of her retaining it is open to two interpretations, and Cristich testified for her. Maurice Cristich! Madame Romanoff! the renowned Romanoff, Maurice Cristich! Have I been pusillanimous, prudent or merely cruel? For the life of me I cannot say!

SOUVENIRS OF AN EGOIST

Eheu fugaces! How that air carries me back, that air ground away so unmercifully, *sans* tune, *sans* time on a hopelessly discordant barrel-organ, right underneath my window. It is being bitterly execrated, I know, by the literary gentleman who lives in chambers above me, and by the convivial gentleman who has a dinner party underneath. It has certainly made it impossible for me to continue the passage in my new Fugue in A minor, which was being transferred so flowingly from my own brain on to the score when it interrupted me. But for all that, I have a shrewd suspicion that I shall bear its unmusical torture as long as it lasts, and eventually send away the frowsy foreigner, who no doubt is playing it, happy with a fairly large coin.

Yes: for the sake of old times, for the old emotion's sake—for Ninette's sake, I put up with it, not altogether sorry for the recollections it has aroused.

How vividly it brings it all back! Though I am a rich man now, and so comfortably domiciled; though the fashionable world are so eager to lionise me, and the musical world look upon me almost as a god, and to-morrow hundreds of people will be turned away, for want of space, from the Hall where I am to play, just I alone, my last Fantaisie, it was not so very many years ago that I trudged along, fiddling for half-pence in the streets. Ninette and I—Ninette with her barrel-organ, and I fiddling. Poor little Ninette— that air was one of the four her organ played. I wonder what has become of her? Dead, I should hope, poor child. Now that I am successful and famous, a Baron of the French Empire, it is not altogether unpleasant to think of the old, penniless, vagrant days, by a blazing fire in a thick carpeted room, with the November night shut outside. I am rather an epicure of my emotions, and my work is none the worse for it.

'Little egoist,' I remember Lady Greville once said of me, 'he has the true artistic susceptibility. All his sensations are so much grist for his art.'

But it is of Ninette, not Lady Greville, that I think to-night, Ninette's childish face that the dreary grinding organ brings up before me, not Lady Greville's aquiline nose and delicate artificial complexion.

Although I am such a great man now, I should find it very awkward to be obliged to answer questions as to my parentage and infancy.

Even my nationality I could not state precisely, though I know I am as much Italian as English, perhaps rather more. From Italy I have inherited my genius and enthusiasm for art, from England I think I must have got my common-sense, and the capacity of keeping the money which I make; also a certain natural coldness of disposition, which those who only know me as a public character do not dream of. All my earliest memories are very vague and indistinct. I remember tramping over France and Italy with a man and woman—they were Italian, I believe—who beat me, and a fiddle, which I loved passionately, and which I cannot remember having ever been without. They are very shadowy presences now, and the name of the man I have forgotten. The woman, I think, was called Maddalena. I am ignorant whether they were related to me in any way: I know that I hated them bitterly, and eventually, after a worse beating than usual, ran away from them. I never cared for any one except my fiddle, until I knew Ninette.

I was very hungry and miserable indeed when that rencontre came about. I wonder sometimes what would have happened if Ninette had not come to the rescue, just at that particular juncture. Would some other salvation have appeared, or would—well, well, if one once begins wondering what would have happened if certain accidents in one's life had not befallen one when they did, where will one come to a stop? Anyhow, when I had escaped from my taskmasters, a wretched, puny child of ten, undersized and shivering, clasping a cheap fiddle in my arms, lost in the huge labyrinth of Paris, without a *sou* in my rags to save me from starvation, I *did* meet Ninette, and that, after all, is the main point.

It was at the close of my first day of independence, a wretched November evening, very much like this one. I had wandered about all day, but my efforts had not been rewarded by a single coin. My fiddle was old and warped, and injured by the rain; its whining was even more repugnant to my own sensitive ear, than to that of the casual passer-by. I was in despair. How I hated all the few well-dressed, well-to-do people who were but on the Boulevards, on that inclement night. I wandered up and down hoping against hope, until I was too tired to stand, and then I crawled under the shelter of a covered passage, and flung myself down on the ground, to die, as I hoped, crying bitterly.

The alley was dark and narrow, and I did not see at first that it had another occupant. Presently a hand was put out and touched me on the shoulder.

I started up in terror, though the touch was soft and need not have alarmed me. I found it came from a little girl, for she was really about my own age, though then she seemed to me very big and protecting. But she was tall and strong for her age, and I, as I have said, was weak and undersized.

'Chut! little boy,' said Ninette; 'what are you crying for?'

And I told her my story, as clearly as I could, through my sobs; and soon a pair of small arms were thrown round my neck, and a smooth little face laid against my wet one caressingly. I felt as if half my troubles were over.

'Don't cry, little boy,' said Ninette, grandly; 'I will take care of you. If you like, you shall live with me. We will make a *ménage* together. What is your profession?'

I showed her my fiddle, and the sight of its condition caused fresh tears to flow.

'Ah!' she said, with a smile of approval, 'a violinist—good! I too am an artiste. You ask my instrument? There it is!'

And she pointed to an object on the ground beside her, which I had, at first, taken to be a big box, and dimly hoped might contain eatables. My respect for my new friend suffered a little diminution. Already I felt instinctively that to play the fiddle, even though it is an old, a poor one, is to be something above a mere organ-grinder.

But I did not express this feeling—was not this little girl going to take me home with her? would not she, doubtless, give me something to eat?

My first impulse was an artistic one; that was of Italy. The concealment of it was due to the English side of me—the practical side.

I crept close to the little girl; she drew me to her protectingly.

'What is thy name, *p'tit*?' she said.

'Anton,' I answered, for that was what the woman Maddalena had called me. Her husband, if he was her husband, never gave me any title, except when he was abusing me, and then my names were many and unmentionable. Nowadays I am the Baron Antonio Antonelli, of the Legion of Honour, but that is merely an extension of the old concise Anton, so far as I know, the only name I ever had.'

'Anton?' repeated the little girl, that is a nice name to say. Mine is Ninette.'

We sat in silence in our sheltered nook, waiting until the rain should stop, and very soon I began to whimper again.

'I am so hungry, Ninette,' I said; 'I have eaten nothing to-day.'

In the literal sense this was a lie; I had eaten some stale crusts in the early morning, before I gave my taskmasters the slip, but the hunger was true enough.

Ninette began to reproach herself for not thinking of this before. After much fumbling in her pocket, she produced a bit of *brioche*, an apple, and some cold chestnuts.

'*V'la*, Anton,' she said, 'pop those in your mouth. When we get home we will have supper together. I have bread and milk at home. And we will buy two hot potatoes from the man on the *quai*.'

88

I ate the unsatisfying morsels ravenously, Ninette watching me with an approving nod the while. When they were finished, the weather was a little better, and Ninette said we might move. She slung the organ over her shoulder—it was a small organ, though heavy for a child; but she was used to it, and trudged along under its weight like a woman. With her free hand she caught hold of me and led me along the wet streets, proudly home. Ninette's home! Poor little Ninette! It was colder and barer than these rooms of mine now; it had no grand piano, and no thick carpets; and in the place of pictures and *bibelots*, its walls were only wreathed in cobwebs. Still it was drier than the streets of Paris, and if it had been a palace it could not have been more welcome to me than it was that night.

The *ménage* of Ninette was a strange one! There was a tumbledown deserted house in the Montparnasse district. It stood apart, in an overgrown weedy garden, and has long ago been pulled down. It was uninhabited; no one but a Parisian *gamine* could have lived in it, and Ninette had long occupied it, unmolested, save by the rats. Through the broken palings in the garden she had no difficulty in passing, and as its back door had fallen to pieces, there was nothing to bar her further entry. In one of the few rooms which had its window intact, right at the top of the house, a mere attic, Ninette had installed herself and her scanty goods, and henceforward this became my home also.

It has struck me since as strange that the child's presence should not have been resented by the owner. But I fancy the house had some story connected with it. It was, I believe, the property of an old and infirm miser, who in his reluctance to part with any of his money in repairs had overreached himself, and let his property become valueless. He could not let it, and he would not pull it down. It remained therefore an eyesore to the neighbourhood, until his death put it in the possession of a less avaricious successor. The proprietor never came near the place, and with the neighbours it had a bad repute, and they avoided it as much as possible. It stood, as I have said, alone, and in its own garden, and Ninette's occupation of it may have passed unnoticed, while even if any one of the poor people living around had known of her, it was, after all, nobody's business to interfere.

When I was last in Paris I went to look for the house, but all traces of it had vanished, and over the site, so far as I could fix it, a narrow street of poor houses flourished.

Ninette introduced me to her domain with a proud air of ownership. She had a little store of charcoal, with which she proceeded to light a fire in the grate, and by its fitful light prepared our common supper—bread and radishes, washed down by a pennyworth of milk, of which, I have no doubt, I received the lion's share. As a dessert we munched, with much relish, the steaming potatoes that Ninette had bought from a stall in the street, and had kept warm in the pocket of her apron.

And so, as Ninette said, we made a *ménage* together. How that old organ brings it all back. My fiddle was useless after the hard usage it received that day. Ninette and I went out on our rounds together, but for the present I was a sleeping partner in the firm, and all I could do was to grind occasionally when Ninette's arm ached, or pick up the sous that were thrown us. Ninette was, as a rule, fairly successful. Since her mother had died, a year before, leaving her the organ as her sole legacy, she had lived mainly by that instrument; although she often increased her income in the evenings, when organ-grinding was more than ever at a discount, by selling bunches of violets and other flowers as button-holes.

With her organ she had a regular beat, and a distinct *clientèle*. Children playing with their *bonnes* in the gardens of the Tuileries and the Luxembourg were her most productive patrons. Of course we had bad days as well as good, and in winter it was especially bad; but as a rule we managed fairly to make both ends meet. Sometimes we carried home as much as five francs as the result of the day's campaign, but this, of course, was unusual.

Ninette was not precisely a pretty child, but she had a very bright face, and wonderful gray eyes. When she smiled, which was often, her face was very attractive, and a good many people were induced to throw a sou for the smile which they would have assuredly grudged to the music.

Though we were about the same age, the position which it might have been expected we should occupy was reversed. It was Ninette who petted and protected me—I who clung to her.

I was very fond of Ninette, certainly. I should have died in those days if it had not been for her, and sometimes I am surprised at the tenacity of my tenderness for her. As much as I ever cared for anything except my art, I cared for Ninette. But still she was never the first with me, as I must have been with her. I was often fretful and discontented, sometimes, I fear, ready to reproach her for not taking more pains to alleviate our misery, but all the time of our partnership Ninette never gave me a cross word. There was something maternal about her affection, which withstood all ungratefulness. She was always ready to console me when I was miserable, and throw her arms round me and kiss me when I was cold; and many a time, I am sure, when the day's earnings had been scanty, the little girl must have gone to sleep hungry, that I might not be stinted in my supper.

One of my grievances, and that the sorest of all, was the loss of my beloved fiddle. This, for all her goodwill, Ninette was powerless to allay.

'Dear Anton,' she said, 'do not mind about it. I earn enough for both with my organ, and some day we shall save enough to buy thee a new fiddle. When we are together, and have got food and charcoal, what does it matter about an old fiddle? Come, eat thy supper, Anton, and I will light the fire. Never mind, dear Anton.' And she laid her soft little cheek against mine with a pleading look.

'Don't,' I cried, pushing her away, 'you can't understand, Ninette; you can only grind an organ—just four tunes, always the same. But I loved my fiddle, loved it! loved it!' I cried passionately. 'It could talk to me, Ninette, and tell me beautiful, new things, always beautiful, and always new. Oh, Ninette, I shall die if I cannot play!'

It was always the same cry, and Ninette, if she could not understand, and was secretly a little jealous, was as distressed as I was; but what could she do?

Eventually, I got my violin, and it was Ninette who gave it me. The manner of its acquirement was in this wise.

Ninette would sometimes invest some of her savings in violets, which she divided with me, and made into nosegays for us to sell in the streets at night.

Theatre doors and frequented placed on the Boulevards were our favorite spots.

One night we had taken up our station outside the Opera, when a gentleman stopped on his way in, and asked Ninette for a button-hole. He was in evening dress and in a great hurry.

'How much?' he asked shortly.

'Ten *sous*, M'sieu,' said exorbitant little Ninette, expecting to get two at the most.

The gentleman drew out some coins hastily and selected a bunch from the basket.

'Here is a franc,' he said, 'I cannot wait for change,' and putting a coin into Ninette's hand he turned into the theatre.

Ninette ran towards me with her eyes gleaming; she held up the piece of money exultantly.

'Tiens, Anton!' she cried, and I saw that it was not a franc, as we had though at first, but a gold Napoleon.

I believe the good little boy and girl in the story-books would have immediately sought out the unfortunate gentleman and bid him rectify his mistake, generally receiving, so the legend runs, a far larger bonus as a reward of their integrity. I have never been a particularly good little boy, however, and I don't think it ever struck either Ninette or myself—perhaps we were not sufficiently speculative—that any other course was open to us than to profit by the mistake. Ninette began to consider how we were to spend it.

'Think of it, Anton, a whole gold *louis*. A *louis*,' said Ninette, counting laboriously, 'is twenty francs, a franc is twenty sous, Anton; how many sous are there in a louis? More than an hundred?'

But this piece of arithmetic was beyond me; I shook my head dubiously.

'What shall we buy first, Anton?' said Ninette, with sparkling eyes. 'You shall have new things, Anton, a pair of new shoes and an hat; and I—'

But I had other things than clothes in my mind's eye; I interrupted her.

'Ninette, dear little Ninette,' I said coaxingly, 'remember the fiddle.'

Ninette's face fell, but she was a tender little thing, and she showed no hesitation.

'Certainly, Anton,' she said, but with less enthusiasm, 'we will get it to-morrow—one of the fiddles you showed me in M. Boudinot's shop on the Quai. Do you think the ten-franc one will do, or the light one for fifteen francs?'

'Oh, the light one, dear Ninette,' I said; 'it is worth more than the extra money. Besides, we shall soon earn it back now. Why if you could earn such a lot as you have with your old organ, when you only have to turn an handle, think what a lot I shall make, fiddling. For you have to be something to play the fiddle, Ninette.'

'Yes,' said the little girl, wincing; 'you are right, dear Anton. Perhaps you will get rich and go away and leave me?'

'No, Ninette,' I declared grandly, 'I will always take care of you. I have no doubt I shall get rich, because I am going to be a great musician, but I shall not leave you. I will have a big house on the Champs Elysées, and then you shall come and live with me, and be my housekeeper. And in the evenings, I will play to you and make you open your eyes, Ninette. You will like me to play, you know; we are often dull in the evenings.'

'Yes,' said Ninette meekly, 'we will buy your fiddle to-morrow, dear Anton. Let us go home now.'

Poor vanished Ninette! I must often have made the little heart sore with some of the careless things I said. Yet looking back at it now, I know that I never cared for any living person so much as I did for Ninette.

I have very few illusions left now; a childhood, such as mine, does not tend to preserve them, and time and success have not made me less cynical. Still I have never let my scepticism touch that childish presence. Lady Greville once said to me, in the presence of her nephew Felix Leominster, a musician too, like myself, that we three were curiously suited, for that we were, without exception, the three most cynical persons in the universe, Perhaps in a way she was right. Yet for all her cynicism Lady Greville I know has a bundle of old and faded letters, tied up in black ribbon in some hidden drawer, that perhaps she never reads now, but that she cannot forget or destroy. They are in a bold handwriting, that is, not, I think, that of the miserable, old debauchee, her husband, from whom she has been separated since the first year of her marriage, and their envelopes bear Indian postmarks.

And Felix, who told me the history of those letters with a smile of pity on his thin, ironical lips—Felix, whose principles are adapted to his conscience and whose conscience is bounded by the law, and in whom I believe as little as he does in me, I found out by accident not so very long ago. It was on the day of All Souls, the melancholy festival of souvenirs, celebrated once a year, under the November fogs, that I strayed into the Montparnasse Cemetery, to seek inspiration for my art. And though he did not see me, I saw Felix, the prince of railers, who believes in nothing and cares for nothing except himself, for music is not with him a passion but an *agrément*. Felix bareheaded, and without his usual smile, putting fresh flowers on the grave of a little Parisian grisette, who had been his mistress and died five years ago. I thought of Balzac's 'Messe de l'Athée' and ranked Felix's inconsistency with it, feeling at the same time how natural such a paradox is. And myself, the last of the trio, at the mercy of a street organ, I cannot forget Ninette.

Though it was not until many years had passed that I heard that little criticism, the purchase of my fiddle was destined very shortly to bring my life in contact with its author. Those were the days when a certain restraint grew up between Ninette and myself. Ninette, it must be confessed, was jealous of the fiddle. Perhaps she knew instinctively that music was with me a single and absorbing passion, from which she was excluded. She was no genius, little Ninette, and her organ was nothing more to her than the means of making a livelihood; she felt not the smallest *tendresse* for it, and could not understand why a dead and inanimate fiddle, made of mere wood and catgut, should be any more to me than that. How could she know that to me it was never a dead thing, that even when it hung hopelessly out of my reach, in the window of M. Boudinot, before ever it had given out wild, impassioned music beneath my hands, it was always a live thing to me, alive and with a human, throbbing heart, vibrating with hope and passion.

So Ninette was jealous of the fiddle, and being proud in her way, she became more and more quiet and reticent, and drew herself aloof from me, although, wrapped up as I was in the double egoism of art and boyhood, I failed to notice this. I have been sorry since that any shadow of misunderstanding should have clouded the closing days of our partnership. It is late to regret now, however. When my fiddle was added to our belongings, we took to going out separately. It was more profitable, and, besides, Ninette, I think, saw that I was growing a little ashamed of her organ. On one of these occasions, as I played before a house in the Faubourg St. Germain, the turning point of my life befell me. The house, outside which I had taken my station was a large, white one, with a balcony on the first floor. This balcony was unoccupied, but the window looking to it was open, and through the lace curtains I could distinguish the sound of voices. I began to play; at first, one of the airs that Maddalena had taught me; but before it was finished, I had glided off, as usual, into an improvisation.

When I was playing like that, I threw all my soul into my fingers, and I had neither ears nor eyes for anything round me. I did not therefore notice until I had finished playing that a lady and a young man had come out into the balcony, and were beckoning to me.

'Bravo!' cried the lady enthusiastically, but she did not throw me the reward I had expected. She turned and said something to her companion, who smiled and disappeared. I waited expectantly, thinking perhaps she had sent him for her purse. Presently the door opened, and the young man issued from it. He came to me and touched me on the shoulder.

'You are to come with me,' he said, authoritatively, speaking in French, but with an English accent. I followed him, my heart beating with excitement, through the big door, into a large, handsome hall and up a broad staircase, thinking that in all my life I had never seen such a beautiful house.

He led me into a large and luxurious *salon*, which seemed to my astonished eyes like a wonderful museum. The walls were crowded with pictures, a charming composition by Gustave Moreau was lying on the grand piano, waiting until a nook could be found for it to hang. Renaissance bronzes and the work of eighteenth century silversmiths jostled one another on brackets, and on a table lay a handsome violin-case. The pale blinds were drawn down, and there was a delicious smell of flowers diffused everywhere. A lady was lying on a sofa near the window, a handsome woman of about thirty, whose dress was a miracle of lace and flimsiness.

The young man led me towards her, and she placed two delicate, jewelled hands on my shoulders, looking me steadily in the face.

'Where did you learn to play like that, my boy?' she asked.

'I cannot remember when I could not fiddle, Madame,' I answered, and that was true.

'The boy is a born musician, Felix,' said Lady Greville. 'Look at his hands.'

And she held up mine to the young man's notice; he glanced at them carelessly.

'Yes, Miladi,' said the young man, 'they are real violin hands. What were you playing just now, my lad?'

'I don't know, sir,' I said. 'I play just what comes into my head.'

Lady Greville looked at her nephew with a glance of triumph.

'What did I tell you?' she cried. 'The boy is a genius, Felix. I shall have him educated.'

'All your geese are swans, Auntie,' said the young man in English.

Lady Greville, however, ignored this thrust.

'Will you play for me now, my dear,' she said, 'as you did before—just what comes into your head?'

I nodded, and was getting my fiddle to my chin, when she stopped me.

'Not that thing,' bestowing a glance of contempt at my instrument. 'Felix, the Stradivarius.'

The young man went to the other side of the room, and returned with the case which I had noticed. He put it in my hand, with the injunction to handle it gently. I had never heard of Cremona violins, nor of my namesake Stradivarius; but at the sight of the dark seasoned wood, reposing on its blue velvet, I could not restrain a cry of admiration.

I have that same instrument in my room now, and I would not trust it in the hands of another for a million.

I lifted the violin tenderly from its case, and ran my bow up the gamut.

I felt almost intoxicated at the mellow sounds it uttered. I could have kissed the dark wood, that looked to me stained through and through with melody.

I began to play. My improvisation was a song of triumph and delight; the music, at first rapid and joyous, became slower and more solemn, as the inspiration seized on me, until at last, in spite of myself, it grew into a wild and indescribable dirge, fading away in a long wail of unutterable sadness and regret. When it was over I felt exhausted and unstrung, as though virtue had gone out from me. I had played as I had never played before. The young man had turned away, and was looking out of the window. The lady on the sofa was transfigured. The languor had altogether left her, and the tears were streaming down her face, to the great detriment of the powder and enamel which composed her complexion.

She pulled me towards her, and kissed me.

'It is beautiful, terrible!' she said; 'I have never heard such strange music in my life. You must stay with me now and have masters. If you can play like that now, without culture and education, in time, when you have been taught, you will be the greatest violinist that ever lived.'

I will say of Lady Greville that, in spite of her frivolity and affectations, she does love music at the bottom of her soul, with the absorbing passion that in my eyes would absolve a person for committing all the sins in the Decalogue. If her heart could be taken out and examined I can fancy it as a shield, divided into equal fields. Perhaps, as her friends declare, one of these might bear the device 'Modes et Confections'; but I am sure that you would see on the other, even more deeply graven, the divine word 'Music.'

She is one of the few persons whose praise of any of my compositions gives me real satisfaction; and almost alone, when everybody is running, in true goose fashion, to hear my piano recitals, she knows and tells me to stick to my true vocation—the violin.

'My dear Baron,' she said, 'why waste your time playing on an instrument which is not suited to you, when you have Stradivarius waiting at home for the magic touch?'

She was right, though it is the fashion to speak of me now as a second Rubenstein. There are two or three finer pianists than I, even here in England. But I am quite sure, yes, and you are sure, too, oh my Stradivarius, that in the whole world there is nobody who can make such music out of you as I can, no one to whom you tell such stories as you tell to me. Any one, who knows, could see by merely looking at my hands that they are violin and not piano hands.

'Will you come and live with me, Anton?' said Lady Greville, more calmly. 'I am rich, and childless; you shall live just as if you were my child. The best masters in Europe shall teach you. Tell me where to find your parents, Anton, and I will see them to-night.'

'I have no parents,' I said, 'only Ninette. I cannot leave Ninette.'

'Shade of Musset, who is Ninette?' asked Felix, turning round from the window.

I told him.

'What is to be done?' cried Lady Greville in perplexity. 'I cannot have the girl here as well, and I will not let my Phoenix go.'

'Send her to the Soeurs de la Misericorde,' said the young man carelessly; 'you have a nomination.'

'Have I?' said Lady Greville, with a laugh. 'I am sure I did not know it. It is an excellent idea; but do you think he will come without the other? I suppose they were like brother and sister?'

'Look at him now,' said Felix, pointing to where I stood caressing the precious wood; 'he would sell his soul for that fiddle.'

Lady Greville took the hint. 'Here, Anton,' said she, 'I cannot have Ninette here—you understand, once and for all. But I will see that she is sent to a kind home, where she will want for nothing and be trained up as a servant. You need not bother about her. You will live with me and be taught, and some day, if you are good and behave, you shall go and see Ninette.'

I was irresolute, but I only said doggedly, feeling what would be the end, 'I do not want to come, if Ninette may not.'

Then Lady Greville played her trump card.

'Look, Anton,' she said, 'you see that violin. I have no need, I see, to tell you its value. If you will come with me and make no scene, you shall have it for your very own. Ninette will be perfectly happy. Do you agree?'

I looked at my old fiddle, lying on the floor. How yellow and trashy it looked beside the grand old Cremona, bedded in its blue velvet.

'I will do what you like, Madame,' I said.

'Human nature is pretty much the same in geniuses and dullards,' said Felix. 'I congratulate you, Auntie.'

And so the bargain was struck, and the new life entered upon that very day. Lady Greville sought out Ninette at once, though I was not allowed to accompany her.

I never saw Ninette again. She made no opposition to Lady Greville's scheme. She let herself be taken to the Orphanage, and she never asked, so they said, to see me again.

'She's a stupid little thing,' said Lady Greville to her nephew, on her return, 'and as plain as possible; but I suppose she was kind to the boy. They will forget each other now I hope. It is not as if they were related.'

'In that case they would already be hating each other. However, I am quite sure your protégé will forget soon enough; and, after all, you have nothing to do with the girl.'

I suppose I did not think very much of Ninette then; but what would you have? It was such a change from the old vagrant days, that there is a good deal to excuse me. I was absorbed too in the new and wonderful symmetry which music began to assume, as taught me by the master Lady Greville procured for me. When the news was broken to me, with great gentleness, that my little companion had run away from the sisters with whom she had been placed—run away, and left no traces behind her, I hardly realised how completely she would have passed away from me. I thought of her for a little while with some regret; then I remembered Stradivarius, and I could not be sorry long. So by degrees I ceased to think of her.

I lived on in Lady Greville's house, going with her, wherever she stayed—London, Paris, and Nice—until I was thirteen. Then she sent me away to study music at a small German capital, in the house of one of the few surviving pupils of Weber. We parted as we had lived together, without affection.

Personally Lady Greville did not like me; if anything, she felt an actual repugnance towards me. All the care she lavished on me was for the sake of my talent, not for myself. She took a great deal of trouble in superintending, not only my musical education, but my general culture. She designed little mediæval costumes for me, and was indefatigable in her endeavours to impart to my manners that finish which a gutter education had denied me.

There is a charming portrait of me, by a well-known English artist, that hangs now in her ladyship's drawing-room. A pale boy of twelve, clad in an old-fashioned suit of ruby velvet; a boy with huge, black eyes, and long curls of the same colour, is standing by an oak music-stand, holding before him a Cremona violin, whose rich colouring is relieved admirably by the beautiful old point lace with which the boy's doublet is slashed. It is a charming picture. The famous artist who painted it considers it his best portrait, and Lady Greville is proud of it.

But her pride is of the same quality as that which made her value my presence. I was in her eyes merely the complement of her famous fiddle.

I heard her one day express a certain feeling of relief at my approaching departure.

'You regret having taken him up?' asked her nephew curiously.

'No,' she said, 'that would be folly. He repays all one's trouble, as soon as he touches his fiddle—but I don't like him.'

'He can play like the great Pan,' says Felix.

'Yes, and like Pan he is half a beast.'

'You may make a musician out of him,' answered the young man, examining his pink nails with a certain admiration, 'but you will never make him a gentleman.'

'Perhaps not,' said Lady Greville carelessly. 'Still, Felix, he is very refined.'

Dame! I think he would own himself mistaken now. Mr. Felix Leominster himself is not a greater social success than the Baron Antonio Antonelli, of the Legion of Honour. I am as sensitive as any one to the smallest spot on my linen, and Duchesses rave about my charming manners.

For the rest my souvenirs are not very numerous. I lived in Germany until I made my *début*, and I never heard anything more of Ninette.

The history of my life is very much the history of my art: and that you know. I have always been an art-concentrated man—self-concentrated, my friend Felix Leominster tells me frankly—and since I was a boy nothing has ever troubled the serene repose of my egoism.

It is strange considering the way people rant about the 'passionate sympathy' of my playing, the 'enormous potentiality of suffering' revealed in my music, how singularly free from passion and disturbance my life has been.

I have never let myself be troubled by what is commonly called 'love.' To be frank with you, I do not much believe in it. Of the two principal elements of which it is composed, vanity and egoism, I have too little of the former, too much of the latter, too much coldness withal in my character to suffer from it. My life has been notoriously irreproachable. I figure in polemical literature as an instance of a man who has lived in contact with the demoralising influence of the stage, and will yet go to Heaven. *A la bonne heure!*

I am coming to the end of my souvenirs and of my cigar at the same time. I must convey a coin somehow to that dreary person outside, who is grinding now half-way down the street.

On consideration, I decide emphatically against opening the window and presenting it that way. If the fog once gets in, it will utterly spoil me for any work this evening. I feel myself in travail also of two charming little *Lieder* that all this thinking about Ninette has suggested. How would 'Chansons de Gamine' do for a title? I think it best, on second thoughts, to ring for Giacomo, my man, and send him out with the half-crown I propose to sacrifice on the altar of sentiment. Doubtless the musician is a country-woman of his, and if he pockets the coin, that is his look out.

Now if I was writing a romance, what a chance I have got. I should tell you how my organ-grinder turned out to be no other than Ninette. Of course she would not be spoilt or changed by the years—just the same Ninette. Then what scope for a pathetic scene of reconciliation and forgiveness—the whole to conclude with a peal of marriage bells, two people living together 'happy ever after.' But I am not writing a romance, and I am a musician, not a poet.

Sometimes, however, it strikes me that I should like to see Ninette again, and I find myself seeking traces of her in childish faces in the street.

The absurdity of such an expectation strikes me very forcibly afterwards, when I look at my reflection in the glass, and tell myself that I must be careful in the disposition of my parting.

Ninette, too, was my contemporary. Still I cannot conceive of her as a woman. To me she is always a child. Ninette grown up, with a draggled dress and squalling babies, is an incongruous thing that shocks my sense of artistic fitness. My fiddle is my only mistress, and while I can summon its consolation at command, I may not be troubled by the pettiness of a merely human love. But once when I was down with Roman fever, and tossed on a hotel bed, all the long, hot night, while Giacomo drowsed in a corner over 'Il Diavolo Rosa,' I seemed to miss Ninette.

Remembering that time, I sometimes fancy that when the inevitable hour strikes, and this hand is too weak to raise the soul of melody out of Stradivarius—when, my brief dream of life and music over, I go down into the dark land, where there is no more music, and no Ninette, into the sleep from which there comes no awaking, I should like to see her again, not the woman but the child. I should like to look into the wonderful eyes of

96

the old Ninette, to feel the soft cheek laid against mine, to hold the little brown hands, as in the old *gamin* days.

It is a foolish thought, because I am not forty yet, and with the moderate life I lead I may live to play Stradivarius for another thirty years.

There is always the hope, too, that it, when it comes, may seize me suddenly. To see it coming, that is the horrible part. I should like to be struck by lightning, with you in my arms, Stradivarius, oh, my beloved—to die playing.

The literary gentleman over my head is stamping viciously about his room. What would his language be if he knew how I have rewarded his tormentress—he whose principles are so strict that he would bear the agony for hours, sooner than give a barrel-organ sixpence to go to another street. He would be capable of giving Giacomo a sovereign to pocket my coin, if he only knew. Yet I owe that unmusical old organ a charming evening, tinged with the faint *soupçon* of melancholy which is necessary to and enhances the highest pleasure. Over the memories it has excited I have smoked a pleasant cigar—peace to its ashes!

THE STATUTE OF LIMITATIONS

During five years of an almost daily association with Michael Garth, in a solitude of Chili, which threw us, men of common speech, though scarcely of common interests, largely on each other's tolerance, I had grown, if not into an intimacy with him, at least into a certain familiarity, through which the salient feature of his history, his character reached me. It was a singular character, and an history rich in instruction. So much I gathered from hints, which he let drop long before I had heard the end of it. Unsympathetic as the man was to me, it was impossible not to be interested by it. As our acquaintance advanced, it took (his character I mean) more and more the aspect of a difficult problem in psychology, that I was passionately interested in solving: to study it was my recreation, after watching the fluctuating course of nitrates. So that when I had achieved fortune, and might have started home immediately, my interest induced me to wait more than three months, and return in the same ship with him. It was through this delay that I am enabled to transcribe the issue of my impressions: I found them edifying, if only for their singular irony.

From his own mouth indeed I gleaned but little; although during our voyage home, in those long nights when we paced the deck together under the Southern Cross, his reticence occasionally gave way, and I obtained glimpses of a more intimate knowledge of him than the whole of our juxtaposition on the station had ever afforded me. I guessed more, however, than he told me; and what was lacking I pieced together later, from the talk of the girl to whom I broke the news of his death. He named her to me, for the first time, a day or two before that happened: a piece of confidence so unprecedented, that I must have been blind, indeed, not to have foreseen what it prefaced. I had seen her face the first time I entered his house, where her photograph hung on a conspicuous wall: the charming, oval face of a young girl, little more than a child, with great eyes, that one guessed, one knew not why, to be the colour of violets, looking out with singular wistfulness from a waving cloud of dark hair. Afterwards, he told me that it was the picture of his *fiancée*: but, before that, signs had not been wanting by which I had read a woman in his life.

Iquique is not Paris; it is not even Valparaiso; but it is a city of civilisation; and but two days' ride from the pestilential stew, where we nursed our lives doggedly on quinine and hope, the ultimate hope of evasion. The lives of most Englishmen yonder, who superintend works in the interior, are held on the same tenure: you know them by a certain savage, hungry look in their eyes. In the meantime, while they wait for their luck, most of them are glad enough when business calls them down for a day or two to Iquique. There are shops and streets, lit streets through which blackeyed Senoritas pass in their lace mantilas; there are *cafés* too; and faro for those who reck of it; and bull fights, and newspapers younger than six weeks; and in the harbour, taking in their fill of nitrates, many ships, not to be considered without envy, because they are coming, within a limit of days to England. But Iquique had no charm for Michael Garth, and when one of us must go, it was usually I, his subordinate, who being delegated, congratulated myself on his indifference. Hard-earned dollars melted at Iquique; and to Garth, life in Chili had long been solely a matter of amassing them. So he stayed on, in the prickly heat of Agnas Blancas, and grimly counted the days, and the money (although his nature, I believe, was fundamentally generous, in his set concentration of purpose, he had grown morbidly avaricious) which should restore him to his beautiful mistress. Morose, reticent, unsociable as he had become, he had still, I discovered by degrees, a leaning towards the humanities, a nice taste, such as could only be the result of much knowledge, in the fine things of literature. His infinitesimal library, a few French novels, an Horace, and some well thumbed volumes of the modern English poets in the familiar edition of Tauchnitz, he put at my disposal, in return for a collection, somewhat similar, although a little larger, of my own. In his rare moments of amiability, he could talk on such matters with *verve* and originality: more usually he preferred to pursue with the bitterest animosity an abstract fetish which he called his "luck." He was by temperament an enraged pessimist; and I could believe, that he seriously attributed to Providence, some quality inconceivably malignant, directed in all things personally against himself. His immense bitterness and his careful avarice, alike, I could explain, and in a measure justify, when I came to understand that he had felt the sharpest stings of poverty, and, moreover, was passionately in love, in love *comme on ne l'est plus*. As to what his previous resources had been, I knew nothing, nor why they had failed him; but I gathered that the crisis had come, just when his life was complicated by the sudden blossoming of an old friendship into love, in his case, at least, to be complete and final. The girl too was poor; they were poorer than most poor persons: how could he refuse the post, which, through the good offices of a friend, was just then unexpectedly offered him? Certainly, it was abroad; it implied five years' solitude in Equatorial America. Separation and change were to be accounted; perhaps, diseases and death, and certainly his 'luck,' which seemed to include all these. But it also promised, when the term of his exile was up, and there were means of shortening it, a certain competence, and very likely wealth; escaping those other contingencies, marriage. There seemed no other way. The girl was very young: there was no question of an early marriage; there was not even a definite engagement. Garth would take no promise from her: only for himself, he was her bound lover while he breathed; would keep himself free to claim her, when he came back in five years, or ten, or twenty, if she had not chosen better. He would not bind her; but I can imagine how impressive his dark, bitter face must have made this renunciation to the little girl with the violet eyes; how tenderly she repudiated her freedom. She went out as a governess, and sat down to wait. And absence only rivetted faster the chain of her affection: it set Garth more securely on the pedestal of her idea; for in love it is most usually the reverse of that social maxim, *les absents ont toujours tort*, which is true.

Garth, on his side, writing to her, month by month, while her picture smiled on him from the wall, if he was careful always to insist on her perfect freedom, added, in effect, so much more than this, that the renunciation lost its benefit. He lived in a dream of her; and the memory of her eyes and her hair was a perpetual presence with him, less ghostly than the real company among whom he mechanically transacted his daily business. Burnt away and consumed by desire of her living arms, he was counting the hours which still prevented him from them. Yet, when his five years were done, he delayed his return, although his economies had justified it; settled down for another term of five years, which was to be prolonged to seven. Actually, the memory of his old poverty, with its attendant dishonours, was grown a fury, pursuing him ceaselessly with whips. The lust of gain, always for the girl's sake, and so, as it were, sanctified, had become a second nature to him; an intimate madness, which left him no peace. His worst nightmare was to wake with a sudden shock, imagining that he had lost everything, that he was reduced to his former poverty: a cold sweat would break all over him before he had mastered the horror. The recurrence of it, time after time, made him vow grimly, that he would go home a rich man, rich enough to laugh at the fantasies of his luck. Latterly, indeed, this seemed to have changed; so that his vow was fortunately kept. He made money lavishly at last: all his operations were successful, even those which seemed the wildest gambling: and the most forlorn speculations turned round, and shewed a pretty harvest, when Garth meddled with their stock.

And all the time he was waiting there, and scheming, at Agnas Blancas, in a feverish concentration of himself upon his ultimate reunion with the girl at home, the man was growing old: gradually at first, and insensibly; but towards the end, by leaps and starts, with an increasing consciousness of how he aged and altered, which did but feed his black melancholy. It was borne upon him, perhaps, a little brutally, and not by direct self-examination, when there came another photograph from England. A beautiful face still, but certainly the face of a woman, who had passed from the grace of girlhood (seven years now separated her from it), to a dignity touched with sadness: a face, upon which life had already written some of its cruelties. For many days after this arrival, Garth was silent and moody, even beyond his wont: then he studiously concealed it. He threw himself again furiously into his economic battle; he had gone back to the inspiration of that other, older portrait: the charming, oval face of a young girl, almost a child, with great eyes, that one guessed one knew not why, to be the colour of violets.

As the time of our departure approached, a week or two before we had gone down to Valparaiso, where Garth had business to wind up, I was enabled to study more intimately the morbid demon which possessed him. It was the most singular thing in the world: no man had hated the country more, had been more passionately determined for a period of years to escape from it; and now that his chance was come the emotion with which he viewed it was nearer akin to terror than to the joy of a reasonable man who is about to compass the desire of his life. He had kept the covenant which he had made with himself; he was a rich man, richer than he had ever meant to be. Even now he was full of vigour, and not much past the threshold of middle age, and he was going home to the woman whom for the best part of fifteen years he had adored with an unexampled constancy, whose fidelity had been to him all through that exile as the shadow of a rock in a desert land: he was going home to an honourable marriage. But withal he was a man with an incurable sadness; miserable and afraid. It seemed to me at times that he would have been glad if she had kept her troth less well, had only availed herself of that freedom which he gave her, to disregard her promise. And this was the more strange in that I never doubted the strength of his attachment; it remained engrossing and unchanged, the largest part of his life. No alien shadow had ever come between him and the memory of the little girl with the violet eyes, to whom he at least was bound. But a shadow was there; fantastic it seemed to me at first, too grotesque to be met with argument, but in whose very lack of substance, as I came to see, lay its ultimate strength. The notion of the woman, which now she was, came between him and the girl whom he had loved, whom he still loved with passion, and separated them. It was only on our voyage home, when we walked the deck together interminably during the hot, sleepless nights, that he first revealed to me without subterfuge, the slow agony by which this phantom slew him. And his old bitter conviction of the malignity of his luck, which had lain dormant in the first flush of his material prosperity, returned to him. The apparent change in it seemed to him just then, the last irony of those hostile powers which had pursued him.

'It came to me suddenly,' he said, 'just before I left Agnas, when I had been adding up my pile and saw there was nothing to keep me, that it was all wrong. I had been a blamed fool! I might have gone home years ago. Where is the best of my life? Burnt out, wasted, buried in that cursed oven! Dollars? If I had all the metal in Chili, I couldn't buy one day of youth. Her youth too; that has gone with the rest; that's the worst part!'

Despite all my protests, his despondency increased as the steamer ploughed her way towards England, with the ceaseless throb of her screw, which was like the panting of a great beast. Once, when we had been talking of other matters, of certain living poets whom he favoured, he broke off with a quotation from the 'Prince's Progress' of Miss Rossetti:

'Ten years ago, five years ago,
  One year ago,
Even then you had arrived in time;
  Though somewhat slow;
Then you had known her living face
  Which now you cannot know.'

He stopped sharply, with a tone in his voice which seemed to intend, in the lines, a personal instance.

'I beg your pardon!' I protested. 'I don't see the analogy. You haven't loitered; you don't come too late. A brave woman has waited for you; you have a fine felicity before you: it should be all the better, because you have won it laboriously. For heaven's sake, be reasonable!' He shook his head sadly; then added, with a gesture of sudden passion, looking out over the taffrail, at the heaving gray waters: 'It's finished. I haven't any longer the courage.' 'Ah!' I exclaimed impatiently, 'say once for all, outright, that you are tired of her, that you want to back out of it.' 'No,' he said drearily, 'it isn't that. I can't reproach myself with the least wavering. I have had a single passion; I have given my life to it; it is there still, consuming me. Only the girl I loved: it's as if she had died. Yes, she is dead, as dead as Helen: and I have not the consolation of knowing where they have laid her. Our marriage will be a ghastly mockery: a marriage of corpses. Her heart, how can she give it me? She gave it years ago to the man I was, the man who is dead. We, who are left, are nothing to one another, mere strangers.'

One could not argue with a perversity so infatuate: it was useless to point out, that in life a distinction so arbitrary as the one which haunted him does not exist. It was only left me to wait, hoping that in the actual event of their meeting, his malady would be healed. But this meeting, would it ever be compassed? There were moments when his dread of it seemed to have grown so extreme, that he would be capable of any cowardice, any compromise to postpone it, to render it impossible. He was afraid that she would read his revulsion in his eyes, would suspect how time and his very constancy had given her the one rival with whom she could never compete; the memory of her old self, of her gracious girlhood, which was dead. Might not she too, actually, welcome a reprieve; however readily she would have submitted out of honour or lassitude, to a marriage which could only be a parody of what might have been?

At Lisbon, I hoped that he had settled these questions, had grown reasonable and sane, for he wrote a long letter to her which was subsequently a matter of much curiosity to me; and he wore, for a day or two afterwards, an air almost of assurance which deceived me. I wondered what he had put in that epistle, how far he had explained himself, justified his curious attitude. Or was it simply a *résumé*, a conclusion to those many letters which he had written at Agnas Blancas, the last one which he would ever address to the little girl of the earlier photograph?

Later, I would have given much to decide this, but she herself, the woman who read it, maintained unbroken silence. In return, I kept a secret from her, my private interpretation of the accident of his death. It seemed to me a knowledge tragical enough for her, that he should have died as he did, so nearly in English waters; within a few days of the home coming, which they had passionately expected for years.

It would have been mere brutality to afflict her further, by lifting the veil of obscurity, which hangs over that calm, moonless night, by pointing to the note of intention in it. For it is in my experience, that accidents so opportune do not in real life occur, and I could not forget that, from Garth's point of view, death was certainly a solution. Was it not, moreover, precisely a solution, which so little time before he had the appearance of having found? Indeed when the first shock of his death was past, I could feel that it was after all a solution: with his 'luck' to handicap him, he had perhaps avoided worse things than the death he met. For the luck of such a man, is it not his temperament, his character? Can any one escape from that? May it not have been an escape for the poor devil himself, an escape too for the woman who loved him, that he chose to drop down, fathoms down, into the calm, irrecoverable depths of the Atlantic, when he did, bearing with him at least an unspoilt ideal, and leaving her a memory that experience could never tarnish, nor custom stale?

Printed in Great Britain
by Amazon